Corrupt City 2

Corrupt City 2

Tra Verdejo

www.urbanbooks.net

Urban Books, LLC
78 East Industry Court
Deer Park, NY 11729

ISBN 13: 978-1-60162-448-2
ISBN 10: 1-60162-448-4

First Printing May 2011
Printed in the United States of America

10 9 8 7 6 5 4 3 2 1

This is a work of fiction. Any references or similarities to actual events, real people, living or dead, or to real locales are intended to give the novel a sense of reality. Any similarity in other names, characters, places, and incidents is entirely coincidental.

Distributed by Kensington Publishing Corp.
Submit Wholesale Orders to:
Kensington Publishing Corp.
C/O Penguin Group (USA) Inc.
Attention: Order Processing
405 Murray Hill Parkway
East Rutherford, NJ 07073-2316
Phone: 1-800-526-0275
Fax: 1-800-227-9604

Acknowledgments

Peace to the Gods and Earths.

I want to thank **YOU (all the readers).** Please continue to support **Tra Verdejo and Street Scriptures,** and I promise I won't let you down. Again thank you for the support. Tell a friend to tell a friend.

Everything I do is to make my mother proud, **Mirta Davila.** I love you. Rest in peace. I want to thank a woman who's been in my life for the past sixteen years, **Dinean "Purefied" Verdejo**. I love you, girl. I know we have struggled, but I won't rest until I make it happen.

Omighty Verdejo, my oldest son, I'm very proud of you. You in the honor roll society and an all-star baseball player. Just keep up the great job and your father got you.

Destin Verdejo, my little man. You are such a bright kid; you amaze me every day with your intelligence. I'm such a blessed man. I have a beautiful family.

I want to thank my father, **Pedro Verdejo.** Without his blood I would be nothing. I want to thank my sisters **Tee, Yazmin**, and **Nichole Verdejo.** My nieces and nephews, **Rae, Destine, Tyler, Nelly,** and **Kenya.**

I want to thank my grandmother, **Carmen Alomar.** I want to thank **Melissa Edwards**, my second mother. I love you.

My street love—I want to thank **Freddy "Tone" Garcia,** my brother for life. I love you. My other brother, **Remy Rich,** from Wagner Projects. My cousin from P.R., **Ruddy**. My other niggas from the block, like **Ray Roc, Daddio, Born Knowledge, Snypes, Smoke, D.B., Inna Terror, Eric,** known as **Last Breath, DJ Kauso, Lizzy Long, Buddha Bride, Ill Murda, Hammer, Mutie, Black Justice, Benell,** aka **Green Eyes,** the whole **Harlem,** especially **Spanish Harlem, 119th Street** and **Lexington Avenue, Wagner Projects.**

My author love—My nigga **Silk White,** we are taking this game by storm. Let's keep getting this paper. We are laughing all the way to the fucking bank. Also, **Carl Weber,** thanks for the shot. The deal almost went sour. **Carl,** you step in and kept your word.

I want to shout out all the authors I break bread with, **Kwame "Dutch" Teague, Tenia Jamilla, Maxwell Penn, Inch, Dashawn Taylor, Rukyyah Kareem, Street Landlords, Jihad, Eisha Brown, Book Banditz, BX Bookman,** and many more.

I also want to thank the whole Baltimore for showing me nothing but love. All the readers who made purchases and shown their support at both my store, Street Scriptures, located at 2609 E. Monument Street, Baltimore, MD, and every weekend at the Patapsco flea market.

I'm sorry if I left any names out. I will get you next time.

To all my haters who are praying on my downfall, yah could kiss my Puerto Rican ass. I don't plan to stop, so step your hating game up.

Table of Contents

Chapter 1

Who Killed the Commissioner?

It was going on seven in the morning when Sergio heard loud bangs on his front door. When he finally woke up, got out of bed, and looked through the peephole, he saw a scary-faced, out-of-breath Lucky standing on the other side of his door. He looked like a crackhead outside of his connect's door, waiting for that hit. At first, Sergio was a bit skeptical about opening his front door. He hadn't seen Lucky since the day before he'd testified in court. Sergio had helped Lucky set up that video swap in that Italian restaurant in the Bronx when his former partners were looking for him and his girl. He was the one who told the detective he called her Chanel because that was her fragrance of choice.

Sergio knew it was bad news, but Lucky had been like a father to him, giving him all the tools he needed to survive on the streets. Sergio did a lot of hits and robberies for Lucky and was basically his dirty hands. Since Lucky was a police officer, he couldn't go around killing people, so he would send Sergio to handle it all. Sergio trusted him with his life. And Lucky had no other place to run to apart from his young protégé.

Sergio couldn't leave him standing out there in distress, so he opened the door.

A fatigued Lucky quickly rushed inside and yelled, "Hurry up! Shut the door, Sergio, and keep the lights off!"

"Okay, but what the fuck is going on?" a now scared Sergio asked.

"How in the fuck did they know about the storage facility? Who in the fuck is snitching? Everything is over, Sergio. These muthafuckas almost killed me," Lucky said as he paced back and forth in the living room. He'd escaped a near-death situation on the rooftop of his storage facility in the Bronx.

"Just calm down and tell me what happened. You need something to drink? Who tried to kill you?"

"Man, these last few days have been hell, and it's only getting worse by the second. Every time I turn around, it seems like my life is in danger. I should have never fuckin' testified. People always want you to say the truth, but in the end, it will always backfire on you. I would be considered untrustworthy in the court of public opinion. I'm tagged with bad luck for life."

"I saw the news about those two dead cops in Cape Cod a few days ago. Once I saw one of your ex-partners' faces, I knew that was you. I can't believe you killed him at the steps of the post office building."

"Those muthafuckas were up there trying to kill my daughter and her mother. I couldn't let that happen. You know how I feel about my family."

"But what the fuck happened at the storage facility? Why did you come back to the Bronx?" a curious Sergio asked.

"I don't know. It all happened so fast. After Cape Cod, I went down to Atlanta. I dropped the family off and came back to finish what I started. When I pulled up to the storage facility and noticed police were watching the spot, like an idiot, I still pulled over and stopped."

Sergio was surprised to hear him make a mistake like that. "So why didn't you keep going?"

"I don't know that, either. I figured, if I go in, I would at least be able to get bigger guns and kill those bastards. Maybe I should have kept going. Don't matter now. I went in, and that's when all hell broke loose. Divine and Pee-Wee were inside. They already knew about the stakeout. They were watching the cops on our cameras. We just loaded up the weapons and got ready for war."

Lucky paused and thought about his good friend getting his head blown off right in front of him on the rooftop. This was the first time he had a chance to mourn his friend.

Sergio picked up on his mood swing. "What's wrong?"

"Divine, he didn't make it."

"Get the fuck out of here! Are you serious? I'm sorry to hear that. I know how close you two were." Sergio embraced him.

"Yeah, they got Divine. We went up to the roof together, and a sniper shot him right in front of me. I was able to locate the sniper, and I took him out. When I was about to go back downstairs and alert Pee-Wee, I heard more gunfire. I ran toward the edge, looked down from the roof, and there were cops all over, so I decided to bounce."

"Shit. I don't blame you. Who do you think snitched about the spot? Maybe it was one of your clients."

"I doubt it. None of the clients knew about my involvement. They all dealt with Divine directly. All they knew was that Divine had friends in the police department, but no one knew it was me. Well, at least, to my knowledge."

Lucky sipped on the tall glass of orange juice Sergio gave him and just sat back and exhaled. He couldn't get over the bad feeling of leaving Pee-Wee like that. He knew in his heart he was wrong. Lucky knew if he hadn't run, he wouldn't be sitting in Sergio's living room.

As Lucky sat there trying to clear his head, Sergio tapped him on the shoulder. "Look, Lucky, the news is talking about the shooting."

They both sat there and heard Destine Diaz's report. Lucky was shocked to see his storage facility on fire. He assumed the cops set the fire to trap and kill him. The news report freaked them out when Destine said Lucky was now in police custody, suffering severe third-degree burns and lying in a coma.

"Wow! These bastards are getting desperate. How in the fuck am I in custody? I wonder what slick move they are trying to pull now."

"They can't be serious. How can they claim you in custody when you're sitting on my damn couch? What are you going to do, Lucky?"

"The media may be hyping the story. That burned-up body laying in a coma has to be Pee-Wee. The cops may think it's me, but once the DNA comes back, they will realize I'm still out here. I need to get to Diamond down in Maryland."

"She's in Maryland? How are you going to get down there? There's too much heat on you."

"All I need is a car."

"Done. How about money? You have any on you? Do you need more?"

"I'm straight. I left Diamond with enough. But I still have to go back to that storage facility."

"Are you crazy? For what?"

"I still have a lot of money and drugs hidden in an underground fireproof safe. Once our clients see this footage about the fire, I'm sure they'll be hunting for me as well."

"Well, just let me know what you need me to do. Anything for you."

"I'm going to need you to go in the storage facility and get my money. I only trust you. We may have to wait a few days, a week or so, but we have to move fast."

"Cool. I'm ready. Just let me know. Hey, Donald, I need to speak to you."

Lucky quickly became suspicious when Sergio addressed him by his government name. He placed his left arm around Sergio, and with his right, he gripped his 9-millimeter parked on his hip.

"What's going on, Sergio?" Lucky asked, praying he wasn't the snitch. "You haven't called me *Donald* in a long time."

"This is going to be my last ride."

"Your last ride?" Lucky removed his hand from the gun, relieved that Sergio wasn't about to reveal anything that would cost him his life.

"I'm homesick. My family in Venezuela needs me."

"Venezuela? I thought you were Dominican." Lucky laughed. "That's cool. I understand. I'm glad you been as loyal as you have been. Once you help me get my money, I will throw in a bonus for you. I love you like the son I never had."

Sergio laughed. "You don't have to, but I'll take it."

They both started laughing.

Lucky sat back on the sofa and tried to continue to laugh, but he couldn't. Not after the night he had. He was beat. If it wasn't for Sergio's presence, he would have broken down like a little bitch. In less than a month, he had killed four people, witnessed his best friends get murdered, lost his operation, had to push away Diamond, reunited with his daughter, and almost lost his life. He was starting to feel like he had worn out his name. Maybe he wasn't so lucky, after all.

Sergio picked up on his daze. "Lucky? Yo, what's up? Snap out of it. You need to start thinking of your next move."

Lucky didn't respond to Sergio's call. He just sat there motionless. He should have listened to Tasha and waited a few days in Atlanta before coming back to New York. That was when he realized he needed to call her.

"Serg, I need a quick favor. I need you to run down the street to a pay phone and call this number. Ask for Tasha and tell her I'm alive and I'm not in custody as they claim. Tell her I will call her soon."

"No problem," Sergio replied as he headed toward his bedroom to change his clothes.

Lucky figured Tasha must have heard about him being in custody and lying in a coma. He wanted to make sure she didn't have a panic attack.

While Sergio was gone, the demons reemerged. Lucky was getting that old itch, that call of freedom. He started snooping around the apartment, looking for Sergio's coke stash. At that particular moment, he didn't care about the twelve-step program. He needed to escape reality. He was growing frustrated with all the current drama. Drugs would be the only answer to his call for help.

Lucky kept coming up with every excuse in the book, just to find a way to break his sobriety. The longer Sergio took, the closer Lucky got to meeting the devil.

About five minutes later, Lucky quickly ran to the sofa when he heard Sergio's keys.

When Sergio walked in, Lucky stood up and asked, "So what happened? What did she say?"

"I can't repeat everything she said, but she was pretty upset. She was happy to hear you were alive, but, man, she let me have it like I was you."

Lucky laughed. "I'm sorry you had to hear that. She begged me not to come up here. She sensed something was going to happen. Again, my bad, but thank you for relating the info."

"It's all good," Sergio replied.

"Hey, listen, you still party?"

Sergio paused and looked into Lucky's eyes. He couldn't believe what he'd just heard. "I'm sorry. Can you come again?"

"You heard me. Do you still party?"

"C'mon, you don't want to go back down that road. I know things have been crazy, but let's smoke some weed or something."

"Sergio, I just need one line. That's all I'm asking for, one line, partner. I have a ton of shit on my mind, and I can't function like this. I need to relax."

"I don't have any in the house, but I could have it here in thirty minutes," Sergio lied, not wanting anything to do with Lucky's self-destruction.

"Fuck it! Never mind. I don't want any visitors. I guess it's not meant to be. I'm just going to try to get some rest and wait to hear what the commissioner has to say in his press conference tomorrow. I'm going to stick around until then before I bounce down to Maryland."

"That's cool," Sergio said, relieved. "You can stay as long as you want."

Sergio was glad he was able to get Lucky to stop thinking about his old habit. He basically saved him from relapsing. He'd witnessed firsthand the way drug abuse was destroying Lucky's life. Right before the Coleman shooting, Lucky was doing badly, sniffing at least five grams a day. The more he sniffed, the more corrupt he became.

While Lucky lay on the sofa with his eyes closed, Sergio went into his room to get dressed. As he was walking out, he tapped Lucky on his shoulder.

"Hey, man, I have to step out and handle a few things and stop by my girl house."

"Okay, that's cool. I'll be right on this sofa. Around what time you are coming back?"

"Around midnight."

"Damn! That long? Well, bring me something to eat."

"Ha! Ha! Diamond is not around to cook, huh? Well, there's food in the kitchen. Don't wait up. I got this little PYT, and she can fuck for hours."

Lucky waved at him and turned back around to try and continue sleeping.

Two hours later, all he kept doing was tossing and turning back and forth on the sofa. He couldn't stop thinking about what had happened a few hours earlier. The ghosts were haunting him. He could still hear Divine's voice in his head. He kept replaying that last moment when he got shot in the head.

Lucky got off the sofa and started doing push-ups, sets of fifty. Forty minutes and three hundred push-ups later, he stopped, feeling good. Dripping with sweat, he jumped in the shower. He figured a nice, hot shower would help him relax and maybe catch some rest, which he needed.

After a half hour in the shower, Lucky came out feeling like a new man. He'd hand-washed his boxers and undershirt, so he came out with just the towel wrapped around his waist. He figured his clothes would air-dry before Sergio got home.

Lucky lay back down on the sofa and closed his eyes. After a few minutes he felt himself dozing off, but every time he was about to knock out, the sound of gunshots kept waking him up and making him jump. He couldn't shake it off.

He stood on his feet and headed toward Sergio's bedroom. He thought maybe lying on his bed would be better. He didn't want to disrespect him and sleep naked, so he looked in his closet and found a robe. When he removed the robe from the hanger, it accidentally knocked down a few shoe boxes. And that was when Lucky noticed Sergio had lied to him. He found at least a half a kilo, maybe more, hidden in his closet. He wasn't upset. He knew why Sergio had lied, and that was understandable.

Lucky quickly put everything back together and closed the closet door, acting like he didn't see the drugs. He threw the robe on and jumped on Sergio's bed.

He was upset at himself for not thinking about sleeping in Sergio's bed earlier. The bed was the most comfortable bed he'd ever lain on. So comfortable, it was impossible to have nightmares. As he lay there, he started thinking about Tamika and her beautiful smile. He kept rewinding her voice in his head, to help him relax. Before he knew it, he was passed out cold and snoring like an old, fat guy.

About a good four to six hours later, around eight o'clock, Lucky woke up. He couldn't believe he had slept for that long. Feeling hungry, he walked to the kitchen and made himself a sandwich.

As he sat at the table, eating, he thought about Diamond, the love of his life. He was hoping he didn't make a mistake by letting her move down to Maryland on her own. He was happy he was going to see her again. Just then, Tasha, his baby mother, popped up in his thoughts.

It was all downhill after that. His happy thoughts didn't last long. He wanted to return home and reunite with his baby girl and live a normal life. The pressure was on, and he felt like he was hauling a ton with every step he took.

Lucky thought about the coke. He tried to fight the thoughts away. He thought about his twelve-step program. He tried to recite the steps in his head, but all he could think about was white lines and the skies. He tried to remember the motivational speeches his sponsor had preached to him, but he couldn't. Addiction was winning the battle.

Lucky was backed into a corner. It was easy for him to stay sober when he wasn't around the drug. He sat down on the sofa, thinking about the Ziploc filled with raw, uncut coca. He quickly stood back up and started walking to the kitchen. Then he made a sharp right down the hallway and entered Sergio's room.

As he reached for the closet door to hit the stash, out of nowhere his daughter, Tamika, popped in his head. He jumped back and landed on Sergio's bed. "What the fuck am I doing?" he asked himself.

As he sat on the bed, flashes of his daughter's innocent face kept running through his mind. He couldn't relapse, for her sake. He walked out of Sergio's room and sat on the sofa and tried to watch a movie.

It didn't take long for thoughts about his partner's death to resurface. Divine was his childhood friend and business partner. He couldn't accept his death, and he blamed only himself. A lot of people were dying around him, and it was fucking with his head. For a second, Lucky thought he was going crazy. He stood up and said, "Man, fuck this!" He walked back into Sergio's closet, grabbed a Ziploc filled with cocaine, and headed back to the kitchen table.

He reached in the Ziploc, grabbed a handful of coke, and threw it on the glass tabletop. He stared at it for at least twenty minutes, fighting the demon within. His body wanted to do it, but his mind was putting up a good fight, but not for long.

Lucky dropped his face in the cocaine like Tony Montana in *Scarface*, sniffing and eating it like a savage. After a few seconds of nonstop action, he leaned his head back and let the high take him over.

Because Lucky had been clean for so long, his body didn't know how to react. He grabbed his head in hopes that it would make the room stop spinning. When he leaned forward, he noticed blood dripping from his nose. He tried to get up and quickly fell back down. He couldn't walk a straight line. The floor felt like an escalator.

He stumbled his way back to the bathroom, knocking lamps over and pictures off Sergio's nightstand. When he reached the bathroom and looked in the mirror, he got spooked. Instead of seeing his reflection, all he saw was blood. That was when he punched the mirror, shattering it instantly.

With blood pouring from his knuckles, Lucky began yelling out loud, "C'mon, muthafucka! C'mon!" He was throwing wild punches into the air. He ran out of the bathroom and closed the door behind him, thinking he was locking the demons in the bathroom.

Instead of him just lying back down on the sofa, he went back to the kitchen table and jammed another mountain of cocaine up his nose. He didn't care about the blood dripping down his nose and lips. His main concern was what was going up his nose. He paused to catch his breath and slapped his body back down on the sofa. He was wasted, incoherent.

Sergio's beautiful white robe was now filled with bloodstains from both Lucky's nose and fist. Lucky's only hope was for Sergio to walk in and save his life. Unknown to Lucky, though, Sergio's girlfriend wasn't letting him go until the morning. He was going to have to ride the nightmare out alone, the whole night.

As he lay on the sofa, trying to let his new high sink in, all he thought about was bullets and dead bodies. He thought about running in a police station and killing everyone. He jumped up and began laughing out loud. "I'm going to get my revenge!" He closed the bloody robe, threw on his shoes, grabbed his rifle, and left.

It was going on almost midnight when Lucky left, wearing nothing but his shoes and a robe. There was no way he would make it far without someone calling 9-1-1 and reporting a maniac running naked, armed with a rifle. He was really testing his luck with that stunt.

The next morning, around eleven o'clock, Sergio walked in his front door and realized something was off when he didn't see Lucky on his sofa. He reached for his gun and slowly started walking around his own house like a burglar. He noticed blood on the floor that led to his bedroom. When he looked in his kitchen, he saw the drugs on his table. He put his gun away, figuring Lucky had found his stash, but he couldn't understand why there was blood everywhere.

He walked into his bedroom calling out, "Lucky? Lucky, you back here, man? Please don't tell me you did what I think you did."

Sergio was shocked to see his room ransacked and Lucky missing. He went to check the bathroom, where he saw the bloody, broken mirror. He knew something was wrong. He ran out his front door and went outside to look for Lucky.

After a good twenty-minute search and coming up empty, Sergio returned home in hopes that Lucky was waiting for him. When he made it back to his apartment and saw no sign of Lucky, he thought the worst.

He looked at his watch and noticed it was going on noon, so he turned his TV on. He didn't want to miss the commissioner's press conference. As he sat there listening to one of the city's most corrupt officials, the unexpected happened. The commissioner was assassinated in the middle of his speech.

Sergio quickly jumped back and placed his right hand over his mouth. He thought maybe he was dreaming because what he'd just witnessed only happened in the movies. He turned the TV off and started walking back and forth in his living room, repeating to himself, "Lucky, where are you?" Sergio's fear was that Lucky was the triggerman.

About five minutes went by and Sergio was still pacing back and forth in his living room. He wasn't answering his cell phone. He was puzzled and didn't know what to think. Was Lucky capable of pulling off such a hit?

An hour went by, and still no sign of Lucky. Sergio spent about half an hour cleaning up the mess Lucky left behind. He ran to the front door when he heard someone knocking, and looked through the peephole, hoping it was Lucky, but it was Roc, one of the neighborhood kids.

He opened the door. "What's good, Roc? Remember, I don't sell weed anymore."

"Man, fuck da bud. I went up to da roof to roll one an' celebrate the death of da top pig, and I found this big-ass rifle up there. Can I hide it in here? Momdukes be flippin'."

"Let me see that gun." Sergio quickly noticed it was the same rifle Lucky had had with him. "Where you said you found this gun at?"

"On the roof. Don't even try to say dis gat is yours. I found it first, son."

"Nigga, shut up!" Sergio almost bitch-slapped Roc. He thought maybe he had something to do with Lucky's disappearance. "This gun belongs to my boy. Show me where you found it at."

When they reached the roof, Roc pointed to where he'd found it. "Right dere, fam. It was right dere."

"Okay, you could leave now."

"What about my—"

"Roc, the fuckin' gun is not yours. Bounce!" He waited as Roc took his time to leave.

Roc wanted to say something slick back but knew that even though Sergio looked like a slouch, he was far from one.

Once Roc left, Sergio began looking around on the roof. The large roof had a tall wall that hid the boiler and water tank.

To his surprise, he found Lucky in a sitting position, leaning back on the water tank. Sergio couldn't believe his eyes. Lucky was naked and using a bloody robe as his sheet. Sergio thought he was unconscious. He ran up to him and got on his knees and shook him awake.

After a few shakes, Lucky came to it. His eyes were open, but he was still a bit woozy.

"Lucky, c'mon, wake up. Let's go back in my apartment," Sergio said as he helped him off the floor.

When they finally made it back to the apartment, Sergio locked his door and windows. He was scared to death.

Lucky was still out of it, but slowly getting back to normal. “What’s going on, Sergio? What time is it? The commissioner should be coming on soon with his speech.”

“Are you serious? You really don’t know what happened?” Sergio asked in shock.

“Seriously. I mean, I don’t know how I passed out on the roof. I mean, I know how, but I don’t know what the fuck you are talking about,” a confused Lucky answered.

Sergio turned his TV on and turned the volume up as high as he could.

Lucky turned toward the TV, and within seconds, he was in disbelief. “Tell me I didn’t see what I just saw. Did someone just assassinate Commissioner Fratt?”

“Someone? You sure it wasn’t you?”

“It wasn’t me, Sergio. I was on the roof, passed out. I don’t remember shit. That couldn’t have been me.”

“It doesn’t matter now. They are going to pin this on you, regardless. You expose corruption in the entire city and cost them millions in lawsuits. They will either kill you or lock you away for life. We need to get you down to Maryland as soon as possible.”

“Sergio, you have to believe me.”

“Lucky, I don’t know what to believe. You wasn’t here when I came home. You left the apartment, coked out of your mind. You don’t even remember what happened yourself, not to mention you up in my place in the process.”

“I’m sorry,” Lucky shot back. He refocused on the issue at hand. “Sergio, how in the fuck I’m going to get out of the city? All the tolls and bridges will be locked down.”

“I have an idea.”

“What’s good, Sergio? Give me something good.”

"Dress up like a woman. I have a costume right here. Don't ask how or why I have it. What do you think?"

"Ha! I like it. Let's do it. I want to leave right now, anyway. This will be perfect."

Lucky wasn't in a position to question his manhood at that moment. Asking him to dress up like a woman a few weeks ago would have gotten Sergio a black eye. He actually thought it was a brilliant idea. He jumped in the shower and got dressed.

Sergio helped him with the makeup, which made Lucky feel uncomfortable.

"Hey, man, you a fag?"

"C'mon, you know me, Lucky. Relax. You know I'm not gay."

"Then you need to explain the costume," Lucky said, backing away from him.

"You think I'm fuckin' gay? Hell no! While you been away in rehab and hiding, I started my own enterprise. I was hired to do a few jobs, and that costume came in handy."

Lucky looked at him up and down. He couldn't do anything but believe Sergio was telling the truth. "My bad. I still had to ask and be sure." He continued to let Sergio apply makeup on him and fix his wig.

Twenty minutes later, Sergio had Lucky looking like a believable woman. He gave him ten thousand dollars, the keys to the car, and a cell phone.

"Call me as soon as you touch Maryland and get with Diamond. I'll figure out a way to get in the storage facility."

"A'ight, cool, but don't go in the storage without speaking to me first. Good looking out for coming through, kid."

"You are like a father to me. Hurry up. Get out of here and be safe."

They embraced each other for a few seconds, both ready to cry, but they held their emotions. They knew it might be the last time they would ever see each other.

"Hey, before I leave, I'm sorry for going through your shit and messing up the crib."

"Don't worry about it."

Lucky grabbed a small black bag and went out the door. He jumped in the car and got on the Cross Bronx Expressway, headed toward the George Washington Bridge. The expressway was stop and go, so it took Lucky a little over an hour to get close to the bridge.

As he got closer, he realized what was causing the delay—checkpoints on every lane. Lucky even noticed dogs going into people's backseats and trunks. *Shit! The dogs would sniff the guns, for sure.*

As Lucky pulled up, he lowered his window and acted dumbfounded, his heart pounding harder in his chest. He didn't want to mess up his rehearsed female voice. "Hello. OMG, what's going on? Did we just have another terror attack?"

"No, miss lady. The commissioner was shot today, and we're looking for the suspect."

"Well, as you can see, I'm traveling alone on my way to visit my mother in New Jersey. Go ahead and search the car."

"I already see you're alone, and I don't need to search the inside of your car, but please pop the trunk, let me look inside, and then you are good to go."

As soon as the officer said "Pop the trunk," Lucky thought about hitting the gas, but it sounded like the cop just wanted to take a peep inside. He hit the button, and the trunk opened automatically.

"Thank you for your kindness, ma'am." As the officer walked toward the back of the car, he called for his partner to bring the dog.

Lucky's heart dropped when the other officer ran over with the dog.

After the two cops spoke for a few seconds, one of them walked back over to the car. "Okay, ma'am, my partner doesn't see the need to have the dog sniff your car. You're free to go."

Lucky thanked the officer and drove off.

Chapter 2

Chaos in the Streets of New York

About an hour after the commissioner was assassinated in front of hundreds of reporters and millions watching live on TV, New Yorkers panicked and began rioting. They didn't know if Lucky was dead or alive, and didn't think it was him.

Many were running and yelling, "We are under attack!"

It was hard for New Yorkers to ever forget 9/11, many still feeling like al-Qaeda would attack again. And the heavy police presence and helicopters didn't help at all, either.

All across the five boroughs, the looters were outnumbering the law. In Brooklyn, there were reports that five officers had been shot, one fatally.

The mayor's office was chaotic, with every phone line ringing. Ralph Gulliano was on the phone with the secretary of defense, Hilda Canton. He was begging for the National Guard to step in and help with the riot. New York was sinking at a fast pace and needed national help.

"We need help down here," an out-of-breath Ralph said. "We have the entire city running wild, and five police officers already have been shot."

"Okay, Mayor, calm down. The president has agreed, and help is on the way. We're dispatching troops from

Fort Hamilton now, and we have more coming from Fort Dix, New Jersey. You do your best until help arrives. General Edgar Thomas will contact you."

"Thank you, and please thank the president for me."

"You can thank him yourself. He will be in New York tomorrow to debrief you."

Ralph hung up the phone. "Fuck me!" he yelled out loud. He was happy to hear about the help but worried about the president's visit. The mayor went in his boardroom, where he met with lead detectives from all divisions across all five boroughs. When he entered the room, he was quickly attacked with questions.

"Who killed the commissioner?"

"What are we all doing here?"

"Calm down, everyone. Right now, our prime suspect is Lucky, but we still don't have any concrete evidence that he pulled the trigger. At first we thought we'd captured him and he was in a coma. This backstabber is still on the lam, and he's our suspect until further notice. We will hold a press conference and blame it on him until we hear otherwise. I need everyone in this room to work around the clock and come up with leads. I need to know what kind of weapon was used to kill Brandon. I just got word military help is on the way, and the president will be here tomorrow. I need some fucking leads on the gun and Lucky's whereabouts before the big guy gets here. Now please, everyone, stop listening and sitting on your ass. Hit those streets and get some answers. I have a riot on my hands, and we need to stop it ASAP."

After they all left the boardroom, the mayor stood in there for about another minute before he left. He wanted to catch his breath and pray to God he could stop the riot before the president arrived.

He headed downstairs to meet with his team of secret agents and the SWAT team. They gave him a bulletproof vest as he entered a military Humvee. He wanted to drive around and see with his own eyes what was going on. He was disappointed to see New Yorkers destroying the city.

Most businesses, some in flames, had their front windows busted in. Every car parked in the street was destroyed, some with pipe bombs. At that particular moment, he felt ashamed to be called a mayor.

After about three hours of driving, the mayor got the call that General Edgar Thomas was already in the city. They agreed to meet on Thirtieth Street and Eleventh Avenue.

The general arrived by helicopter. The mayor was surprised at the quick response, but he was happy. He needed the experienced personnel. He didn't have any experience in handling a riot.

When the mayor came out of the Humvee to greet the general, he was shut down.

"How are you doing, General? I'm Mayor—"

"I know who you are. You're the asshole who can't run his city quietly! I'm in New Jersey, training the finest men for combat before they deploy to Iraq. I don't want to be here, but since I am, let's get straight to the point. I have three thousand soldiers on their way, and we don't have time to waste."

"So you know my police commissioner was assassinated, and now the city has gone mad and they are running wild in the streets?"

"Don't worry. I will restore order. My men should be here shortly. Please alert your police department to arm their men with rubber bullets and Tasers. When we hit the streets, we are sweeping through them, and we are hitting every idiot who doesn't obey. Make sure the media is out there with us. Once word gets out we are shooting everyone with rubber bullets, we should have order restored by the morning."

The mayor waited a few seconds to respond. He wanted to make sure he understood the general clearly.

"Let me get this right. You want to run through my city with three thousand troops shooting rubber bullets?"

"Affirmative. Any problems, take it up with the president tomorrow."

They all entered the Humvee and headed back down to One Police Plaza to regroup and strategize on a plan to regain control of the city. When they arrived, the governor joined the team, and they worked rigorously.

After reviewing the little bit of facts they had, they decided to divide the troops up. They sent nine hundred troops each to Brooklyn, the Bronx, and Harlem, two hundred and fifty to Queens, and fifty to Staten Island. Queens and Staten Island were the only two boroughs where the disturbance was at a minimum and not a major threat.

While the soldiers were deploying to different boroughs, the mayor grabbed the governor's arm and pulled him to the side. "Are you sure this is the right decision? We're about to hit the streets and just start shooting people. Also, do we need those water cannon tanks?"

"They are only rubber bullets. We don't have a choice," the governor fired back.

"I still think it's the wrong move. I pray God helps us all," the mayor said.

They walked back toward the general and entered one of the many water cannon tanks. Those water cannons shot two hundred and fifty pounds of pressure per minute and were the perfect weapon for riot control. The mayor decided to stay in Manhattan along with the governor and the general.

Out of the nine hundred soldiers, five hundred were sent to Harlem while the other four hundred headed toward Chinatown and Delancey Street. As they were moving along the streets, you could hear the shots being fired into the crowds and the screams right after.

Both the mayor and governor had concerned looks on their faces. Hearing the loud screams of the people made them both think they might be making a mistake.

The general picked up on their weakness and tried to lift their spirits. "I don't know why the long faces, gentlemen. In a few hours you will have control of the streets again."

"I just hope those rubber bullets don't kill anyone."

"Don't worry. They won't. Get ya tail out ya asses!"

They didn't respond to the general's remarks, as they kept looking out the window in disbelief. When they reached Delancey Street, it was a mess, with most of the stores in flames or broken into. And people were running out of stores with stolen merchandise.

At first the rowdy crowd was hesitant to obey the military warning to stop rioting and return home, but once the rubber bullets started flying, they all scatted like roaches. As hard as it was for the mayor and governor to admit, the general's plan looked like it was working.

Within three hours they were able to mobilize most of downtown Manhattan, but Times Square was a different story. The beautiful lights were now dimmed, and the place was in flames, with thousands of people running around, destroying everything in sight.

"General, when are we going to use these damn water cannons?" the mayor yelled.

"You must have read my mind. I'm giving the order now."

The general looked at the mayor and grinned slightly. He finally grew balls, he thought.

As the two hundred and fifty pounds of pressured water was fired into the crowd, folks dropped to the ground like flies. The mayor's worries were gone as he saw the crowd running away in fear. The mayor asked the general for an update on the troops in the other boroughs.

Five minutes later, the general told the mayor, "Well, the troops in Harlem are experiencing difficulties. The urban community is fighting back with real bullets, and a few soldiers were injured, but none fatally. As far as Brooklyn, they're still experiencing major issues as well. Three more police officers have been killed, over a dozen soldiers were shot, and three were burned severely. We have about ten civilians confirmed dead."

"What the fuck! How did that happen?" the mayor asked.

"Listen, I can't provide details. I'm just giving you an update. These civilians are shooting at my troops."

"I thought we were only using rubber bullets. How did the civilians get killed?"

"Mayor, c'mon, our troopers are discharging rubber bullets, but since civilians are using live ammo, we have to return fire as well. But, according to my intel, not all fatalities were caused by gunfire. You should consider most of these civilians lucky."

"Lucky? Please, General, don't you ever say that word in my presence."

As the general was about to respond, the governor jumped in.

"General, the guy possibly responsible for the assassination of the commissioner goes by the name of Lucky. He is also responsible for starting this riot."

"I understand. Well, when all this is over, if you need my assistance in capturing this Lucky character, just give me a call. Anyway, let's get back to work. That way we can head up to Harlem as soon as possible and help the other troops."

Lucky had caught the city by surprise, and so far he was winning and getting away with everything.

As they headed up to Harlem, the mayor started thinking about Lucky. He couldn't help it. He was actually thinking like a man who had been through a twenty-round fight with Mike Tyson. He was drained and couldn't come up with any new strategies to capture him. He decided he was going to follow up on the general's offer to help catch Lucky. He knew the longer they took in restoring the peace, the farther away Lucky was getting. He wanted to end this before the morning. That way he could find out who killed his commissioner.

When they arrived in Harlem, they saw that the situation was under control. There were still a few idiots running around, but the threat had been eliminated. It didn't take the Harlem residents long to realize they weren't going to beat the army.

The mayor called Richard on his cell phone. "Hey, where do we stand with Lucky's apprehension?"

"Nothing yet. We shut down all the bridges and tunnels. No one can come in or out, and we are searching every suspicious car."

"At what time did you shut everything down?"

"Right after the soldiers came in. Why?"

"Maybe he slipped through before the shutdown."

"That's not possible. Right after the assassination, we were already checking every car, bus, and truck before the shutdown."

"If he's still in New York, his ass is mine. Meet me back at One Police Plaza."

"Okay. You sound like everything is under control. Did the general's plan work?"

"Yes, ninety percent of the riot has been stopped. We had a few civilian casualties and more police officers that were shot and killed."

After the mayor hung up the phone, he turned around and shook hands with the general. He'd doubted him at first, but his plan worked. The mayor and the governor jumped out of the tank and got in a waiting black Suburban. They wanted to get back to work on capturing Lucky as quickly as possible.

On their way downtown, the governor asked, "Do you really think Lucky is capable of pulling off a stunt like that?"

"Yes, I do. After what took place at the storage facility, I'm sure he knows we are gunning for him. He just wanted to strike first. I'm not surprised at all."

The rest of the fifteen-minute drive downtown was silent as both men were in their own world, thinking about their next move. The mayor was worried about the president's visit, and meanwhile the governor was going through the list of candidates to replace the mayor.

Lucky was frustrated and puzzled. Because of traffic, it took him seven hours to get to Maryland, when it should have taken only three to four. What really had him stressed was the fact that he was dressed like a woman, making the whole ride uncomfortable.

Lucky was ready for a nice shower and a home-cooked meal when he pulled up to the house in Maryland. But he didn't see Diamond's car, and the house looked like it was abandoned.

Automatically, he knew something was wrong. He was going to keep driving, but then he remembered he was dressed up like a woman. He parked and got out of the car. Folks in the neighborhood would think he was just looking at the house with plans of buying it.

He walked up to the house, and his suspicion was on point. Diamond had never made it to the house.

He walked back to his car and sat there for a few minutes to think about his next move. He was worried for Diamond. He wondered what had happened to her, if was she still alive. He leaned his head back and closed his eyes, and the tears almost dropped down his cheek.

Lucky didn't know where to turn. He needed to check into a hotel, but he couldn't use his ID.

He drove down Robert Crain Highway and stopped at the first gas station. He went in the bathroom, which to his luck was coed. He ripped off the costume and washed the makeup off his face. When he was done, he asked the gas attendant for the nearest mall.

He grabbed his black bag after parking the car because he didn't intend to use the car again.

Five minutes later, Lucky was walking through Marley Station Mall in Glen Burnie, walking around looking for a female victim, planning to get her drunk so she could use her ID for a hotel room.

After a ten-minute walk, he found his victim. He saw two girls walking out of Victoria's Secret. The fat, ugly girl was holding a large bag, and the pretty, petite girl was holding a small bag. Lucky thought it should have been the other way around because big girls shouldn't shop in Victoria's Secret.

He approached the two girls. "Excuse me, sweet ladies." He turned to the pretty girl. "Can I ask why you are only holding a little bitty bag?"

The two girls were a bit annoyed by Lucky's interruption, but when they got a good look at him and they saw his biceps, they both were mesmerized.

"I didn't see anything I liked in there."

"What's your name, love?"

"My name is Janay, and that's my friend Peaches. What's your name?"

"My name is Donald. Tell your friend Peaches you will be right back."

"Peaches rolls with me everywhere," Janay said.

"Listen, baby girl, I just want to go back in Victoria's Secret and pick out a few things I would love to see you in. Don't worry about the price. I got it."

Janay went silent. She didn't know what to say. No man had ever approached her the way Lucky just did. Plus, she wasn't honest about why she was only holding a small bag. She just didn't have the funds.

Peaches tapped her on the arm. "You better go on with that man, girl. I will see you later. Call me."

After Janay and Lucky walked in Victoria's Secret, they were quickly told they had about thirty minutes until closing time.

"Listen, baby girl, go grab whatever you want. My favorite color is red."

"Is that right? I love red, too. I see we have some things in common."

"That's why I approached you. How about after we shop, we go get a few drinks and find out how much in common we have?"

She licked her lips. "Sounds like a plan."

Lucky knew he had her from the way she was looking him up and down. After Janay picked up a few outfits, perfumes, and body mist, she was ready to go.

"That's all you want, baby? We still have about ten more minutes before they close."

"I'm good. I'm ready for some drinks, though."

As they left the store, Lucky put his hands around her and asked, "Where can we eat and drink around here?"

"Where you from? I know you not from Maryland. You have a New York accent."

Lucky laughed. "Is it that obvious?"

"Yes, it is, but I love it. It's a turn-on," a flirty Janay said.

"Let's hurry up and get these drinks in our system. That way you could tell me what else turns you on."

They both looked at each other seductively, like they were ready to rip each other's clothes off.

Janay thought quickly and said, "I'm parked by the front. Where is your car?"

"Let's go in your car, sweetie. My brother dropped me off while he handled his business. I was shopping for an outfit. He's taking me out to a club."

"Oh, word? What club?"

"I think it's called Love. It's in D.C."

"Yeah, I've been there. You will love it."

"I heard. I didn't even find an outfit. I'll just wear something I brought with me. I was going to call a cab, until I seen your pretty face."

"Awww, so sweet. I'm assuming a cab is a taxi, right?"

"What do y'all call them out here? Just *taxi?*"

"We just call them *taxi*. In Baltimore they call them *hacks*."

"Hacks? I'm not going to ask. Anyway, we're in your town, so you pick the spot where we are going."

"In Maryland, we are known for our crabs. Do you eat crabs?"

"Yeah, I do. I love seafood."

As they walked to Janay's car, Lucky was surprised to see she was pushing a red 2005 Ford F-150.

"Damn, girl! I would have never thought you was pushing a truck. You look more like a Honda Civic type of girl."

They both laughed as they got in the truck and made their way out of the parking lot, headed to Romano's, an Italian restaurant known for their crab cakes and mixed drinks.

When they arrived, they had to wait about twenty minutes to get seated. Lucky didn't want to sit by the bar because of the TVs nearby. He didn't want to risk his face appearing on the screen. They waited by the front door and took the chance to get to know each other.

"Tell me about you," Lucky said as he got close to Janay. He had to work fast to get her to a hotel.

"Well, I'm single, and I work full-time, no kids, and I like to have fun. How about you, daddy? What do you do?"

"I'm a street dude, and I do street things to survive."

"I kind of figured that, the way you were balling at the mall. I thought you were either a street hustler or a ballplayer, but your face doesn't look familiar, so I knew you must have been a street hustler."

They both started laughing again.

Lucky also learned something new about Janay. She was a gold digger.

They were finally called to be seated, and right off the bat, Lucky ordered two double shots of Hennessy and two Long Island iced teas.

"How you know I like Henny?" she asked, a smirk on her face.

"Reading a person is a gift of mine, but if you would like something else, that would be fine, too."

"Henny is fine, but Long Islands I rarely drink because they get me too horny."

"Oh, word? Then I should cancel the Henny and tell the waiter to keep the Long Islands coming."

Janay started laughing, but Lucky was dead serious.

About an hour and eight drinks later, Lucky and Janay were all over each other like a married couple. They were both drunk, so they were ready to fuck each other's brains out.

Lucky ordered two more shots of Henny and whispered in Janay's ear, "After we finish these two last drinks, let's get out of here. I'm ready to taste you."

"I thought you would never ask," Janay replied, squeezing his big biceps.

"Where is the nearest hotel?"

"Hotel? We could just go to my house," she replied while kissing him.

"I think a hotel would be better. I would feel more comfortable. I don't want any of your old boyfriends popping up."

"You are silly, but there's a Holiday Inn right down Ritchie Highway."

"Let's go then."

They both got up after finishing their drinks and headed back to Janay's truck. It took only about five minutes to reach the hotel. When they reached the front, Lucky gave her two hundred dollars and told her to book a suite.

When they got in the room, it was on like game time as soon as they entered. Lucky jumped on her and started ripping her clothes off. At first he'd just wanted to use her for her ID and to book a room, but after spending time with her, he realized he really wanted to fuck her. He didn't even give her time to change into the red Vicky Secret she picked out. They were too drunk to remember it. They just wanted to have hot, steamy sex.

After about two hours of licking, sucking, slapping, fucking, hair pulling, and choking, Janay lay on the bed like a beaten slave. Lucky had rocked her world and put her ass to sleep.

That was all Lucky was waiting for. He wanted to go downstairs and log on to the Internet. He'd been in the dark on what was going on in New York since he'd left. Janay had done exactly what he wanted her to do—get his mind off things—but now he needed to get back on point.

He walked up to the counter in the lobby, where a young lady sat half asleep. He told her his room number and asked to pay for another night. He knew the sleepy worker wouldn't ask for ID.

He then logged on to the Internet and couldn't believe his eyes. The pictures alone told the story, but Lucky still decided to click on one of the reports. He was shocked to read about the military sweeping through the streets, using rubber bullets and water cannons. He also read that thousands were hospitalized and arrested. Even a few police officers and civilians were killed. Though everything he read was disturbing, he was pleased to read that the mayor had control of at least 90 percent of the city.

Lucky was no innocent angel. He knew that. But some of the articles he read were hurtful. The media kept hinting that he was responsible for the assassination and igniting a riot.

Lucky was pissed at himself for sniffing all that coke and passing out. He hated the fact that he couldn't remember what happened that night. He wanted to believe he didn't pull the trigger, even though he knew he was capable of pulling it off.

After spending about thirty minutes browsing the Net, he went back up to the room and saw Janay sitting up on the bed, looking sad.

"What's wrong, baby girl?"

"Nothing now," she replied, her whole mood switching and a smile on her face.

"You thought I left, right? What kind of dudes you fuck with out here? I went to use the Internet."

"I'm not going to lie. I thought you bounced on me. But what kind of thug logs on the Internet?"

"An organized thug, baby."

Lucky jumped back in the bed, and they went for a quick round two.

Janay had to be at work early, and it was going on four in the morning. Around four thirty, she decided it was time to bounce. "Daddy, I have to leave. I have to be at work in, like, four hours. When can I see you again?"

"I'll be back real soon. I got your number. I will keep in touch."

"Sounds like a plan. I'll call you when I get my lunch break."

They kissed for five more minutes, Janay jerking him off all the while. She got his dick rock hard again and decided to give him a quick blow. She really sucked the shit out his dick. She wanted to make sure all he thought about was her and her skills.

After a long ten minutes of vacuum service, Lucky came all in her mouth, and Janay didn't miss a beat. She kept sucking until the last drop of cum was in her mouth and down her throat, swallowing like a veteran.

Lucky walked her to the door. He slapped her on her ass and said, "Baby girl, I will be thinking about you all day."

After Janay left, Lucky turned on the TV and browsed through the news channels. To his surprise, his face was all over the screen, along with the riots. It almost felt like he was still in New York, with all the coverage he was receiving. That made him nervous because he'd clearly shown his face when he walked through the mall and when he was eating at the restaurant. He figured he would just stay in the hotel room for his entire stay. Meanwhile, he would have to figure out a way to reach Tasha down in Atlanta. He was now regretting that he'd tossed the woman's costume at the gas station.

While he was lying on the bed, he thought about Diamond and wondered where the hell she was at. It didn't make sense. Why would she run away?

Lucky thought about numerous scenarios. He thought she either went back to Hunts Point in the Bronx to look for her pimp or she went back home. Both scenarios seemed dumb, but that old saying came to his head. *You could never turn a ho into a housewife.* Lucky laughed out loud and said, "Especially not a recovering hooker. They're liable to make you lose everything and make you fall flat on your face."

Lucky quickly got serious. He jumped off the bed, dropped down to his knees, spread his arms like wings, and began to ask, "Why?"

He asked the question a few more times and then started insulting himself. "How can you be so stupid? You dumb, pussy-whipped bastard!"

It finally hit him that Diamond had set him up. He started punching the walls until his fists began to bleed again. The wounds from breaking Sergio's mirror were still fresh, so blood started flowing rather quickly. Lucky was mad at himself because it took him so long to realize where the knife in his back came from.

He calmly sat on the edge of the bed and rubbed his head. The feeling was almost like the day when his mother died in that horrible car accident. Diamond meant everything to him. He did lie and deceive her, but he would have never double-crossed her. What she did was unforgivable. She obviously wanted him dead and out of the picture.

Lucky was more concerned about her motives and why she fucked him. He felt like he'd been played by his own student.

With Captain Tuna and Speedy still in jail, and a dead commissioner, Lucky had a new mouse to chase. Diamond became his number one target. He still couldn't get over the way she'd crossed him. *You got me, bitch, but please don't let me find you. Please don't*, he thought to himself.

As the morning went on, he kept watching TV, trying to get things off his head, but he couldn't. Around nine in the morning he decided to finally try and get some sleep. He made it a point to stay away from watching the news channels, so he watched ESPN. He didn't want to hear anything else about the riots or the assassination. By nine thirty, he was knocked out cold.

Chapter 3

The Day after the Riots

By ten in the morning, there were numerous news reports hitting all the TV outlets, newspapers, and the Internet, basically still reporting about the aftermath. Everyone was giving the mayor praise for how quickly he defused the riot and got things back in order. At first, city officials were a bit skeptical, especially with the military enforcement and their shoot-first strategy. They thought there were going to be a lot more casualties. Regardless, it was going to cost the city millions of dollars to repair the damage caused by the riot.

A lot of hardworking folks lost their lifelong dreams right before their eyes. It was sad to see so many businesses destroyed. New Yorkers were so upset and caught up in the drama, they didn't realize they were destroying the same stores where they shopped for groceries and household needs. The same stores they would go into with their children and buy school clothes and medicines. The same restaurants they would have family dinner nights at. All of those community stores where you were known by your first name when you entered were the first to be destroyed.

No one ran up in a courthouse and tore that place up, or in a police station and slapped a few police officers for their corrupt behavior, two places where the major corruption was taking place. New Yorkers felt the need to destroy their own communities. Now, instead of just walking down the streets for some eggs and bread, they had to walk for miles in search of a grocery store that was open. New Yorkers started to feel like fools.

And now, instead of supporting Lucky, the whispers around the city were loud and clear. Lucky was to blame for everything.

Just then Destine Diaz's report was about to come on with the latest update.

"Good morning, New York. Today I have to be honest. I really don't feel too proud to be a New Yorker. My drive to work this morning was heartbreaking. Tears were flowing as I was driving. I couldn't believe my eyes. I'm still not over the fact that our police commissioner was assassinated during live taping.

"I know we all want to believe Lucky is responsible for the assassination, but we have not yet heard an official statement from the NYPD. I also want to salute our great mayor and governor for their courage. They actually were out in the streets of New York helping our military troops cease the riot. I also want to thank the many New Yorkers who volunteered their time to help clean the streets this morning. We have a long road ahead of us, and the only way to recover from this tragedy is by working as a whole. We need to show the rest of the world that New York always has been and always will be one of the greatest cities in the world.

"The president is in town, and he's meeting with both the mayor and the governor. I'm sure they will come up with a formula that will rapidly help us recover. There will be a private press conference scheduled right after the meeting with the president. Only two cameras will be allowed to record and broadcast, no reporters. One of those cameras will be one of ours.

Once we have a confirmed time, we will broadcast the press conference. Until then, please let's refocus our attention on rebuilding. Destine Diaz, Channel Five, broadcasting live from One Police Plaza."

Most of the city agreed with Destine's statement about rebuilding its image. City officials had major issues on their hands. They were still dealing with the aftermath of the commissioner's assassination, they still had two of their own locked in Central Booking, facing numerous felonies, Lucky was still unaccounted for, and now he had become one of the fiercest sought-after felons in New York's history.

The government and police department, still embarrassed after they realized Lucky was never in a coma, wanted to capture him in the worst way. Lucky's name was being mentioned in the same breath as bin Laden's.

Lucky's testimony had helped the prosecution build a strong case against the city and police department, and the cops on trial were going to get charged with Coleman's death, destroying the city's good image.

Those five envelopes Lucky had mailed out to the press and lawyers were going to cost the city more millions. The city was facing two major lawsuits for the unlawful arrest and incarceration from the Rell Davis and Juan "Pito" Medina case. The scandal with Cardinal Joseph King III was causing major embarrassment for the church community. New York went from the city of big dreams to one big nightmare.

The recovery process looked like it was going to take years. But then something happened. About thirty minutes after Destine's report, New Yorkers made it their business to speed up the process, and thousands of volunteers hit the streets and began cleaning up, with people of different ethnic backgrounds pitching in—blue-collar workers, Wall Street stockbrokers, and even street-corner hustlers.

America witnessed what happened to New Orleans after the Katrina ordeal. The government didn't care two fucks about the people or their lost property. The insurance companies basically created the expression *Bail out*, going missing as soon as it was time to pay. New Yorkers were not about to let the same thing happen to their city. Everyone came together and began the rebuilding process. Their only hope was that the government didn't bail out on them as well.

While the city was hard at work, Mayor Ralph Gulliano was a nervous wreck because he was going to have his one-on-one with the president in ten minutes. After their initial meeting, he would allow the governor to come in while they strategized on their next move, which was now a federal matter.

When it finally came time to meet President Bernard Osama, the mayor almost pissed his pants. First, the Secret Service came in his office and looked around for about fifteen minutes, making sure there were no hidden cameras.

The president walked in with his million-dollar smile. "How are you doing, Mayor Gulliano?" He extended his hand to greet the mayor.

"I'm doing okay, I guess. It's an honor to be speaking to you, sir," the mayor said as he shook his hand, smiling and acting like a little groupie. "Please, sit down, Mr. President. Can I get you some tea, sir?"

"No, thanks. Let's get down to business. I don't have time to waste."

"Where do you want me to begin? Because, if you want to hear the story from the beginning, it's going to take some time," the mayor said in fear, hoping he didn't offend the president.

"You're right. Just tell me what I need to know and what else you need. I've been informed the military support was a success. What leads do we have on this former cop you guys keep calling Lucky? Do we have facts he actually pulled the trigger yesterday?"

"You are correct, Mr. President. The military presence helped out tremendously. We were able to stop the riot and gain control. Right now, we have no leads on who killed the commissioner, and Lucky hasn't been seen since we raided his storage facility a few days ago."

"Wait a minute. Are you saying no leads and no Lucky?"

"That is correct, sir."

"No wonder the city of New York lost its morals and self-dignity. The people don't feel comfortable following a government with no sense of direction. I'm embarrassed to even be sitting here having this conversation. I'm still trying to figure out a way to stop the war in Iraq and bring our troops home. I don't have the time or the manpower to spare to help fix your problems. Are we clear?" The president asked just to make sure the mayor was paying attention.

"Yes, we are clear, sir," the mayor quickly responded.

"I know the governor is working closely with my office in providing federal help, but I'm going to bring in two agents, ex-Navy SEAL guys, from Washington D.C. They will catch Lucky for you. They are arriving as we speak. I expect my guys to be brought up to speed on everything. With regards to rebuilding New York, don't worry about the cost. FEMA will take care of it. We won't drop the ball like we did in New Orleans. New York is one of the greatest cities on this planet. I want this rebuilding process expedited."

"With all due respect, Mr. President, we don't need any more wild cowboys running around looking for Lucky. We tried that, and it was unsuccessful."

"I understand your concerns, but quite frankly, you are in no position to reject any help. This is bigger than you and I. Don't you see the message we are sending across the world? We can't tolerate assassinations live on TV. What's next? A mayor? Governor? Or even the goddamn president?" the president said, raising his voice and heading toward the door. "This meeting is over. Mrs. Canton will be in contact. I expect full details on your progress. I want this situation taken care of or that's your ass. Have a good day, Mr. Mayor."

The mayor just sat there, frightened like a little kid after his father just finished yelling at him.

As soon as the president left, the governor ran in. "What happened in here? The president didn't look happy," the governor said.

"Everything I expected. It started out nice and calmly, but then he started talking about what if they assassinated us as well, two Navy SEAL guys are coming to help, live TV assassination. I mean, all kinds of crazy shit, and also my ass is on the line. I have a few more days to catch Lucky, because the world is watching."

"What? Slow down, Ralph. Please sit down and repeat yourself, but in English."

The mayor sat down, caught his breath, and counted to ten before opening his mouth again. "The president said he's sending two ex-Navy SEALs to help catch Lucky, and I have a few more days to do it, or that's my ass. But I do have good news. He gave me his word that millions will be available to rebuild New York."

"That's great news. New Yorkers will be happy to hear that. I'm concerned about those two agents he's sending in, but at this point, we need all the help we can get. We don't even know if Lucky is still in New York."

Just as the mayor was about to reply, his secretary came in and said he had a call. The mayor gave her the evil eye for barging in like that, but he knew it must have been important.

"I'm sorry to come in like that, but you have to take this call."

"If it's not the president, take a message."

"Mr. Mayor, I have the Arundel Police Department on the line. They're located in Maryland. Lucky has been spotted at a Holiday Inn hotel."

Both the mayor and governor jumped up when they heard Lucky had been spotted.

The mayor took the call after his secretary left and pressed the speaker button. "This is Mayor Ralph Gulliano. It was brought to my attention you have some information on the whereabouts of one of our fugitives."

"Good day, Mr. Mayor. My name is Captain George Sneed from the Arundel County Police Department down in Maryland. We received a call from a young lady who claimed she met the suspect in question at a mall, and that after they had dinner and drinks, they then proceeded to rent a room at the Holiday Inn in Glen Burnie."

"Captain Sneed, have you dispatched any units to the hotel as of yet?" the mayor asked.

"That's a negative. The young lady claimed they were there only for one night and they both left in the morning. However, she did state she left first."

"I will bet my career he's still at the hotel. He used her for her ID in order to book the room. Call the hotel and have them run the girl's name and see if the hotel stay has been extended. If so, dispatch a few units over there and please call right back. This is my cell number, 646-555-1212. I also need you to call the mall and get in touch with security and ask to review their cameras. I'm sending some of my guys down as well."

"I don't think that would be necessary. We can handle the situation."

"Listen, Captain, this is the governor. I'm also on this call. Three minutes ago the president walked out of here, giving us the green light to apprehend this suspect at all costs. Get off your high horse. Call the hotel and mall like we asked, and we will see you soon."

There was about a three-second pause before Captain Sneed responded, "I will call you as soon as I hang up with the hotel."

Annoyed, the mayor ended the call without saying good-bye. "The nerve of him! Lucky would destroy his bullshit police department."

Both the mayor and the governor were making calls on their cell, trying to get a team together to send down to Maryland. Right in the middle of all the drama, the two agents the president had sent walked in the room.

As the mayor was about to introduce himself, Captain Sneed called his cell phone.

"Mr. Mayor, according to hotel staff, the room was extended for an extra night. I didn't want to alarm the hotel, but I did make the manager aware of the situation. He said that the suspect is still in his room and had just ordered room service."

"That's great news. Dispatch a few units."

"I already have."

"How many?" the mayor asked.

"I sent one, and I have about another five units that would be there within minutes as well."

"Great. Listen, he's extremely dangerous and smart. He will shoot on sight, so please tell your boys to be careful. I will have agents down there within four hours, but I will call my friends over in Baltimore and ask for their help as well."

"You are going to call the Baltimore Police Department? We don't work with those pigs. They are giving us all a bad name."

"Listen, to even come close to catching Lucky, you are going to need cops who are known for getting dirty. I don't have time to worry about a beef between police departments. Thank you for the call."

After the mayor hung up his cell, he introduced himself to the agents. "Hello, fellas. Please tell me your names."

A black, muscular brother, about six-two, head shaved clean, with numerous tattoos around his neck and arms, said, "My name is Special Agent Marquis Jenkins, sir."

"My name is Special Agent Angel Mendez, sir," a five-nine Hispanic brother said. His long black hair was in a ponytail, and he also was tattooed.

Usually, the mayor would have been turned off by their looks, but in this particular situation, this was a perfect fit. Even though Captain Tuna and his boys were dirty, clean-cut guys would get killed easily. In order to fight dirt, he had to get dirty.

"Okay, listen, fellas, we have intel that Lucky is in a hotel room down in Maryland. He may be there for only one night. It will take us about four hours to get there."

"Not if we fly. We flew here, and it only took about an hour," Special Agent Jenkins said.

"Then that settles it. You two fly down to Maryland. My secretary will provide all the information you need. Remember, fellas, shoot to kill on sight."

After the two Secret Service agents left, the mayor looked at the governor and said, "I hope we catch this son of a bitch once and for all."

"I agree. I think we should just let those two agents handle it. We don't need to send anyone else. Plus, our department has suffered enough embarrassment. We don't need to add any more. If that police department doesn't want to work with our Baltimore team, then so what?"

"You're right. Besides, we have a funeral to plan for the commissioner."

The mayor sat there and thought about it for a few. Captain Sneed was right about the Baltimore Police Department being pigs. He remembered when the commissioner was alive and his unit worked with the Baltimore unit. The commissioner had returned from his trip with all sorts of negative comments on their tactics. They had numerous police shootings similar to Perry Coleman's. Innocent, unarmed black men were getting killed, and the cops involved were slapped with desk duties at best.

One particular case stood out in the mayor's mind. A suspect involved in a high-speed car chase with police hit and killed a police officer in the process. The very next morning the suspect was found dead in his jail cell, and no charges were filed against the CO on duty. The mayor wondered how they were able to pull that off.

The city of Baltimore was run by numerous corrupt commissioners, some of whom were charged and fired. You mentioned the word *corruption* to any Baltimorean, and they would tell you, "You must be talking about my town." So it made sense why Captain Sneed was hesitant to work with the Baltimore Police Department.

Chapter 4

The Holiday Inn

Lucky decided to walk over to the hotel gym, which was on the same floor as his room. He wanted to make sure he stayed in shape because running from the law was harder than a marathon. When he got there, no one was using the facility, so he felt comfortable working out. He didn't like the big glass windows in the gym, which gave a clear view of the front of the hotel.

After about thirty minutes of lifting, he decided to jump on the treadmill and run a few miles. While running, he noticed a police cruiser pulling up with flashing lights. He quickly jumped off the treadmill, ran toward the corner of the gym, and peeked out one of the big windows. When he saw two police officers jump out with their guns drawn and running toward the entrance of the hotel, he knew they were there for him.

He ran as fast as he could to his room, grabbed one of his guns and money, and headed toward the stairwell. As he was going down the flight of stairs, he heard one of the officers running up the stairs. He assumed the other cop jumped in the elevator.

Lucky stopped, dropped to one knee, and pointed his gun. Once the officer made that turn toward him, he was going to shoot him. Lucky figured the way those cops had the guns drawn, they were coming to kill him. The officer didn't have any idea what was waiting for him at his next turn.

Once Lucky saw the officer make that turn, he let off two rounds from his 9-millimeter at the officer's chest. The impact of both shots knocked the officer backwards, slamming his body against the wall and dropping him down a flight of steps. As soon as he hit the floor, Lucky was right on top of him. He took his gun, extra ammo, and his radio. Right before he left, he kneeled down to the young officer and whispered in his ear, "I knew you were wearing a vest." Then he got up and continued running down the stairs.

There was a lot of commotion in the lobby, especially after everyone had seen the two officers running in with their guns drawn. Also, the sound of gunfire had the entire hotel concerned. Once everyone saw Lucky busting out the stairwell with a gun in his hand, they started running and screaming for their lives, while ducking at the same time.

Lucky ran out the front door and noticed a guest pulling up. He ran up to the driver's side and opened the door. He pointed the gun at his head and yelled at him, "Get the fuck out or lose your life!" As the nervous driver was exiting his car, Lucky shot out the tires of the police cruiser.

Once the guests at the hotel heard more gunfire, a mini stampede broke out.

As the other police officer was able to make his way through the crowd and reach the front door, he saw Lucky jump into a blue Nissan Maxima. He yelled out, "Freeze!"

But Lucky was already peeling off, so the officer began firing his weapon, and within seconds, Lucky was out of his sight.

The officer called the dispatcher. "Officer down, officer down! I need a bus. This is Officer Lenny Wilson. Suspect has fled the scene in what looked like a dark blue four-door sedan. He disabled my unit by shooting out the tires. I discharged my weapon four times at the suspect, but I missed the target. He made a right out of the hotel. He may be heading towards 895 North."

"This is dispatcher twenty-one. I have already dispatched a bus and alerted all units. We are also contacting the transit department. Are you injured?"

"No, but I believe my partner is. I heard two shots inside the hotel, and my partner is not picking up his radio."

"Please, stand by as help is on the way."

Lucky was listening to the whole conversation. He did make a right, but made the first U-turn available, and pulled into the first shopping center to his right. He parked behind Pizza Hut and jumped out of the blue Nissan.

As soon as he parked, he ran across the parking lot and saw a man in his early twenties about to exit his white 325i BMW. Lucky approached the young driver right before he was about to exit the car and pistol-whipped him before he even knew what happened. He was passed out cold in the backseat of his car.

Lucky got in the driver's seat and peeled off from the parking lot. He made a right, then continued driving on Ritchie Highway. He was listening to the police radio and heard that the cops were still looking for him in a dark blue Nissan. He figured he had at least thirty minutes before they found the Nissan.

Lucky also heard two Secret Service agents were arriving by jet. That was surprising, but he knew it only meant that not only was the federal government involved, but now the president had officially joined the hunt. That made him nervous because soon the CIA would come in the picture. "Damn! Now the alphabet boys are really after me," he whispered under his breath, referring to all the government agencies known only by initials, like the ATF, DEA, FBI, CIA, and even the IRS. Once you were wanted by those agencies, the chances of not getting caught were zero to none.

Lucky knew he couldn't drive all night with a white dude passed out in the backseat. He began making turns at different streets, not knowing where to go. He knew he had to get rid of the car, so he was just waiting to pass the next big shopping center. That way, he'd at least have a little bit of time to steal the car he wanted without the owner in it.

While on Crain Highway he pulled up to a big enough shopping center. He thought it was the perfect spot to find a car. He drove to the farthest part of the lot and parked the BMW. He walked around and noticed there were no security guards present and no outside cameras in sight. Lucky was amazed at how easy it was going to be to steal a car in the plaza. Wanting to play it safe, he walked around just to make sure.

Once he stole his next car, he didn't want any additional attention. He just wanted to be able to jump on I-95 and head back up to New York. He walked over to the Sunoco gas station, and right before he entered, someone approached him.

"What's going on? I got some good green."

Lucky paused, looked at the young kid, and smiled. "What's good, li'l man? Are you sure you got some fire?"

"All you have to do is follow me back to my apartment. I got vicks for thirty-five, halfs for seventy, and onions for one-forty."

"I'm not driving. I live right across the street," Lucky said, pointing at the complex across Crain Highway.

"You live in Village Square? That's what's up. I just came from there. One of my regular customers lives there. I could drive you to your car. Then you could just follow me. I'm like five minutes from here. I live in Hidden Wood apartments."

"My wife has the car. How about I give you an extra fifty dollars if you take me and then bring me back?"

The young hustler looked at Lucky up and down and quickly became suspicious. "How about I just bring it back once you show me where you live? What you need?"

"Listen, I know you don't know me and shit. I don't know you, either. I just need a favor, that's all. I will snatch an ounce off you, plus give you fifty dollars for your trouble. I just want to get high. Your call. I'm trying to be your new number one customer in Village Square."

Lucky said all the right things the young hustler wanted to hear. Buying an ounce plus fifty was easy money.

"A'ight, I don't usually do shit like this, but I'm going to look out for you. C'mon, my car is parked by the pump."

Lucky caught the break he was looking for. He could hide out at the young hustler's crib for a day or two. He just had to play it smooth. When they got in the car, Lucky didn't waste time in sparking a conversation.

"What's your name, young homie?"

"Haze. Everybody calls me Haze. What about you?"

"Donald. Everybody calls me Don. Haze, let me ask you this. What the fuck is a vick? You said you had vicks for sale?"

"A quarter is seven grams. Michael Vick's jersey is number seven. In Maryland, we call a quarter a vick. Where are you from? You sound like you from Up Top."

"Yeah, I'm from New York."

"What part?"

"I'm from the Bronx. You been up there before?"

"I go up to New York all the time. That's where my connect lives. We almost here. I live in these apartments right here."

Lucky had a decision to make when he got upstairs to Haze's apartment— kill him or make him part of his team. He didn't have a lot of options, or too many friends. Once he smoked a few blunts with Haze, then he would make the call. If Haze was a real cat and about his business, then Lucky might have to take a risk on him. In reality, he didn't have any other options.

When they got in the apartment, Haze asked him, "You fuck with Henny?"

"Yeah, I drink, but let's roll up and get high first."

An hour later, they both were leaning back on the sofa, high as a kite, watching the movie *Heat*. In that one hour, Lucky had enough information on Haze to take the risk. He knew li'l man wasn't scared of the police or to bust his gun. Lucky was about to commit suicide with the next move he was about to pull, but he had to take his chance. The kid earned the opportunity by his whole swagger, but if li'l homie didn't agree to roll with the plan, he was going to put a bullet through his head.

"Listen, Haze, turn the movie off and put it on the news for a second."

"News?" Haze laughed. "I don't watch those gay-ass shows."

"I want to show you something. You want to know who I really am, put it on the news."

Haze's facial expression changed. He knew it had to be serious. He turned the movie off and switched it to cable. He pressed GUIDE and surfed the local news channel. While searching, he asked, “What’s on the news?”

“I want you to know who I am.”

“Now you making me think I made the wrong decision by bringing you to my crib,” a serious-faced Haze said.

“Maybe, but if you built like I think you are, everything will be okay.”

After locating the news channel and watching it for less than a minute, Haze realized he’d just smoked with the most wanted man in New York, maybe in America. They were reporting the shooting that took place at the Holiday Inn.

As soon as Lucky noticed Haze finally knew his identity, he pulled out his gun and cocked it back. “Now you have a decision to make, Haze. I don’t want to kill you. If I did, I would have done it when we first came in.”

“So what the fuck you want?”

“I need a little help, like a place to stay for a day or two. You look like a down nigga, so you let me know. Are we good? Can I trust you?”

“Hell yeah, we are good. You like a fucking legend. Everybody is looking for you, and you here in my crib getting high with me. Whatever you need from me, you got.”

“I’m going to put my gun away. Are you sure you straight?” Lucky asked.

“I will be, once you put that bullshit-nine millimeter away.” Haze laughed.

Lucky lowered his gun and began laughing with Haze, but still was trying to read him. He knew he’d picked the right person.

“What you know about guns, li’l man?”

“I’m not on your level yet, sniping muthafuckas, but I got guns.”

"I didn't kill the commissioner. I was set up."

"Word? What about that girl they said you killed right in front of the police station? Did you really kill your female protégé like they say you did? That was an ill move, better than the commissioner hit."

"Well, I did kill that girl, but she wasn't who they thought she was. They were looking for Diamond, who's my real protégé. I needed to clear her name. I made up the story of her turning herself in. Then I shot her right in front of the police station."

"You see, I knew it. You are ill. Yo, I want to roll with you," an overeager Haze said.

"Slow down, Haze. This is not a video game, fam. This is real shit. I got federal agents hunting for me. If they catch me, they are going to kill me. You feel me?"

"I feel you, but do you feel me? I'm a ride-till-I-die muthafucka. This is what I do all day, every day. I smoke weed, make money, and I keep my guns clean."

Now Lucky was beginning to become a bit nervous. He was starting to sound like DMX in that movie *Belly*, when he played an out-of-control thug with an ego bigger than life. He almost second-guessed his decision to pick Haze. He thought he was acting immature, or maybe he was just happy to be around a real criminal. It was time to start testing the little dude.

"Have you ever shot anyone with one of your clean guns?" Lucky asked sarcastically.

"I haven't shot or killed anyone. I been to the range a few times, and I know I could shoot."

"Haze, I'm talking about real cowboy shit. Real blood and dead bodies. Are you up for the task?"

"I'm up for it. This is what I been waiting for my whole life. I'm a thug, yo, you hear me? I'm not like these other cats. I got like six thousand in the closet and another five at my mom's crib. In total, I got four guns, big joints, too. I don't have any kids or a wifey. I have shit to lose."

"I can't front. I'm a little impressed. I busted a lot of hustlers, and most of them fronted like they had money. When we raided their house, we would find like fifteen hundred dollars. Right now, I just need to call my man in New York. He's our contact and our only hope of sneaking into New York safely."

"Are we going to New York?" Haze asked, wide-eyed.

"Slow down with the whole *we* thing. I still haven't decided if you rolling. All I said was I was impressed," Lucky said, messing with him.

"C'mon," Haze pleaded, "you know you need the help."

"Let me just call my man. We'll talk after this phone call."

Lucky reached for his black bag and got the cell phone Sergio gave him and called him.

After a few rings, Sergio picked up. "Lucky, is that you?"

"Yeah. What's up?"

"Where in the fuck are you? There were reports they had you blocked in a hotel and that you shot a cop. Luck must love your black ass."

"It was Diamond, that fuckin' bitch. She was the one who snitched us out."

"Diamond, nah. Are you sure? Not her. I can't believe it."

"When I got down to the house in Glen Burnie, it was empty. She never went to Maryland. The bitch took the money and ran, and put the boys on me. I guess she figured out I was never coming back."

"I guess she figured one hundred thousand was enough to start a new life."

"I don't know about a new life, but it sure cost her her life."

"Where are you? Are you safe?" Sergio asked.

"Yeah, I should be good for a day or two. I'm coming up there, though."

"Up here? Are you crazy, Lucky? Turn the news on. The fuckin' president was up here and made a statement about capturing you. Stay as far away as you possibly can. New York is too hot."

"I don't give a fuck. I still have unfinished business. I'm not running for life. I need you to get in contact with Pee-Wee's brother—his name is Blood—and get me his number. Did you find a way to get my money?"

"I'm working on it."

"A'ight, call me back with Blood's number."

"Lucky, I have followed your orders for years. All I'm asking is this once you consider my advice. Don't come up to New York right now. Lay low and chill."

"Just get me the number and call me back. This is not the time to stick your chest out. It's my life, and I'm making the call. I'm not scared of dying. I'll be waiting on your call."

"Okay."

Lucky hung up the phone. He was upset, which clogged up his thought process. It was hard for him to admit it, but he had to agree with Sergio. He couldn't go back up to New York right away. That was when Haze's apartment came in the picture. Haze could make all the moves for him while he stayed inside and out of sight. He was just nervous that Haze might run his mouth, not to the police, but to his friends.

Lucky walked back toward Haze.

"Okay, look, Haze, I'm going to give you a shot and see how you roll. I need to stay here for like three days. I'd rather stay in a hotel, but I just had to shoot my way out of one. When I go up to New York and everything goes right, I will give you twenty-five thousand dollars."

"Twenty-five thousand? Shit! For that kind of bread, you could sleep in my bed."

They both laughed and shook hands. Haze, eager to prove he was a real thug, would have done it for free, just for the rush of it.

As they rolled up a few more blunts, Lucky began filling him in on his current plan. He didn't waste time on the past because he didn't think it needed addressing.

"Look, li'l homie, from this point on, what we talk about stays between us. If you leak this information, I will kill you, and I'm not even joking. I used to run a storage company, and we stored large quantities of drugs and monies for the mob and kingpins. About eighty percent of the drugs that came up to New York was stored in my storage facility. Then, like many drug corporations, there is always a snitch within the team. The bad part about the snitch is, it was my girlfriend. We got raided, they killed two of my guys, and I escaped. The storage was burned to the ground. I need to get back in the storage because I have an underground stash room with a couple million. I'm going back up to New York to retrieve my money and get some payback on this bitch for snitching. Everything sounds easy, but there will be bloodshed."

"Sounds like a plan. I'm down. And don't worry, yo. I won't run my mouth. I barely hang with niggas. All I do is get money and fuck bitches."

"That's another thing. You can't have company over while I'm here. We can't take chances."

"But I have customers who come to this apartment," Haze quickly shot back.

"Well, when your customers come, I will go into your room while you handle your sale. I don't care about that. I'm talking about having anybody over. That includes bitches."

"That's cool. As long as I can serve and make my money, then I don't have no problem with that."

They continued to smoke and talk. Lucky, at that point, was leaning back and enjoying his high. His mind drifted off, and he started thinking about Diamond. He was puzzled by her betrayal. In his mind, she crossed the line of death. He had to kill her, but he was going to ask her why first. He needed to know why.

Lucky knew she didn't act alone and that maybe there was another man in the picture. He had his suspicions, but he was going to have to wait till he got back up to New York.

He also started thinking about his baby mother, Tasha, and daughter, Tamika. He wanted to call them, but if he did, they would try to persuade him to return to Atlanta. Hearing their voices wouldn't help the situation. Tasha would just have to understand that when he got back to Atlanta. He couldn't give up just yet.

Haze tapped Lucky on his shoulder, interrupting his thoughts.

"Hey, I have a customer who's about to come in here in like two minutes."

"Get that money, li'l homie," Lucky said as he walked toward Haze's bedroom.

While Haze was handling his business, Lucky lay on the bed and started thinking about his daughter again. He couldn't wait to get back to her. He had already lost a lot of years and wasn't about to add to the count. He wanted to settle down and become a father, something his mother could be proud of. He knew he'd been living a life his mother would have never approved of, and imagined her to be flipping in her grave.

Lucky had gotten away from his original home upbringing. After joining Captain Tuna's team, he really turned for the worse, losing all his morals. He'd joined the force to change the stereotype that black people from the hood had about becoming a cop. He wanted to prove that you could come from the hood and be a great officer, not a sellout, like everyone thought.

Lucky was getting tired, and as soon as he closed his eyes, he fell asleep.

Chapter 5

America's Most Wanted

The mayor was upset when he heard that Lucky had escaped and shot a police officer in the process. He'd warned the police department down in Arundel County that Lucky was considered armed and dangerous and would shoot first. He couldn't believe Captain Sneed didn't take him seriously. One of his deputies almost died for his foolish mistake. He got on the phone, called up his new help, and asked for an update.

"Agent Jenkins, are you guys in Maryland yet? What the hell is going on?" a furious mayor asked.

"Mister Mayor, we're at the scene Lucky escaped from. I'm assuming he knew he was wearing a vest and that's why he took the shot. We found the car he hijacked less than a mile away, in a shopping plaza, abandoned. I'm sure he stole another car. They are reviewing security cameras as we speak. Once we find the car he jumped in, we will hunt him down. I will keep you posted."

"Hurry up and find this cocksucker," the mayor said as he hung up.

The mayor didn't need the extra publicity because, in reality, the whole world was laughing at him. He couldn't catch one individual who tore his city apart and killed his commissioner live on TV.

Not more than five minutes after the mayor hung up the phone, the governor called, asking for an update as well. Lucky had escaped so many traps, they were starting to feel like they were wasting their time chasing him.

Aside from all the drama, today was the funeral of one of the mayor's best friends, Commissioner Fratt. With all the recent events taking place, it was going to be hard for the mayor and the rest of New York to feel any sorrow or pain for the commissioner.

As thousands of police officers marched alongside the white stretch Cadillac hearse, the streets weren't crowded. Many New Yorkers were still rebuilding their homes and businesses. They could care less about the corrupt commissioner, who might have been responsible for the worst riot in New York history.

The funeral was one of the quickest and quietest funerals ever for a city official. His wife and kids were stunned that not many of his close friends attended the funeral. Many felt embarrassed to show their support, another indication that they believed he was indeed dirty. The mayor didn't even stay till the end. The city had bigger issues calling for his attention.

The mayor headed back to his office to meet up with his spokesperson, Richard. He needed to get a few updates, and he still had to deal with the whole Captain Tuna and Speedy situation. They were still sitting in lockup at the Booking, in private cells. For their protection, it was best to keep them in Booking rather than transfer them to Rikers Island. The protective custody unit at Rikers had one of the highest murder rates of all the prisons in the United States. They didn't want to take a chance at both Tuna and Speedy getting murdered.

After the mayor arrived back at his office, he told his spokesperson, "Okay, Richard, lay it on me. What have you been hearing down in Maryland?"

"Well, let's first talk about the budget situation. We need to get in contact with the president or someone in FEMA. We're running out of money, and we still haven't received one dollar from those millions they promised."

"How much have we spent so far?" The mayor didn't really want to know the answer.

"In less than forty-eight hours, we have spent a little over ten million dollars, and we still haven't helped the small businesses and the residential community. At this rate, we'll be broke in thirty days. Experts are predicting it will take at least a year to fully recover from the riot, but if we run out of money, it could take three to five years."

"I will make the call. What else?"

"Well, we have to address the whole Tuna and Speedy situation real soon. I heard Internal Affairs is working on both of them. I received confirmation that Internal Affairs feels like Speedy will run his mouth and cooperate. We have to monitor that situation and make sure Speedy remembers which side he's on. At this point, we don't need any more leaks.

"I spoke to the DA. They're willing to give Tuna and Speedy plea deals for the Coleman case. Instead of murder, they will be charged with manslaughter. I don't know how we could get them out of this mess. They're both looking at a minimum of ten years."

"Ten years, Richard? We can't do better than that?"

"Not with the kind of heat and pressure New York is under. We're under a microscope. If they receive a slap on the wrist, it will slow up the healing process in the city. I'm sorry to say, but we're going to have to use those two as examples. And we can't wait until we capture Lucky, either. We need to get them in court as soon as possible."

The mayor sat there in silence because he knew what Richard was trying to imply. He basically was asking him to turn his back on the situation and let the system take its course. That was a hard pill to swallow because he believed in the code of blue, death before betrayal.

The mayor knew he would receive harsh criticism from the police department and the union, but he had to go with his gut feeling, which was following Richard's plan for the moment and seeing where it led. If he had to make a last-minute decision, he would, but at the moment, he was going with the flow.

"Fuck it, Richard! Advise the DA we will accept any deal on the table for the Coleman case. I'll head down and speak to Tuna and Speedy myself."

"I don't think that would be a wise decision, Your Honor. I will have their lawyers break the news down. If they don't cooperate, we pull the plug on their funds and completely abandon them."

"Great idea! Have their lawyers tell them. Also, did anybody find that girl? What's her name again?"

"Who? Diamond?"

"We need to find this girl. She's the final piece in capturing Lucky. Once we put her face and her real identity in the news, he will be rushing back to New York, and we will be waiting," the mayor said with conviction.

"I like that plan. We need to find her quickly. With regards to Lucky, the parking lot cameras captured him jumping in a white BWM after knocking out the driver. They were unable to get the license plate number, but they're running a check on all BWMs in Glen Burnie. A white BMW was spotted in another plaza a few miles down. When officers arrived on the scene, the white car was gone. Right now, they have no leads. I hope those two agents the president provided come through in the clutch because right now we need a game-changing play," Richard said.

"We don't have any leads on Lucky. That's not good. He could be on his way to Mexico, for all we know."

Before Richard could answer, the mayor's secretary barged in the office and informed him that there were two men in suits outside his office. The mayor, along with Richard, headed out of the office to see which agency was now snooping in their business.

"Good day, Mister Mayor. My name is Special Agent Scott Meyer, and this is my partner, Special Agent Marie Summit. We are with the Central Intelligence Agency."

"The CIA!" the mayor said aloud. "First the FBI, now the CIA. Who's next? NASA?"

"We apologize for the inconvenience, but how long did you think we were going to mind our business? When a commissioner gets assassinated live on TV, it becomes our problem."

"The president didn't mention anything about the CIA getting involved."

"The president? You think we're governed by the president? When Commissioner Fratt got assassinated, you invited every terrorist to an open party. We're the nation's first line of defense. We put our country first and the agency behind self. We are here to resolve and stabilize the situation," Agent Meyer said.

"You guys are going to help capture Lucky as well?" The mayor sounded desperate.

"Can we please continue this conversation in your office? And your answer is no. We are here to really find out who killed the commissioner."

"But Lucky killed him," the mayor snapped.

"Based on our intelligence, he's not a suspect."

The room quickly got quiet because, up to that point, Lucky was the prime suspect. When Agent Meyer said Lucky was not a suspect, it made the mayor and his spokesman nervous.

"What are you trying to imply? That his assassination was an inside hit for hire? But who else would dare to pull off such a hit?"

Agent Summit stepped in front of her partner. "That's a question we would love to ask you, sir."

"Excuse me. You better watch your mouth, young lady," an angry mayor said.

Agent Summit reached for her briefcase and pulled out a folder. The mayor took one of those long swallows because he didn't know if the folder she was holding was sent by Lucky. When Lucky had sent those folders out exposing all the corruption, the mayor's name never popped up. He was worried that now his luck had also run out and that he would now be exposed.

Agent Summit threw the folder on his desk. "Then please explain why you made two payments of one hundred thousand dollars from your private offshore account. The first payment was made a day before the assassination, and the second one right after."

The mayor looked through the papers in silence.

Richard was shocked to hear about the new allegations against his boss. "Boss, is this true? You were involved in the assassination?" Up until then, there had been no secrets between them.

The mayor didn't answer his good friend of over twenty-five years. He just kept looking through the folder, which not only contained his bank statements, but also phone records between him and the hired helped, one of the mob's best hit men.

Richard didn't allow the mayor to continue ignoring him. He slapped the folder out of his hands. "You are going to answer me right now! Answer me, goddamn it! Is it true? Is it true?"

The mayor, too embarrassed to admit he was the one who actually ordered the hit on the commissioner, kept his silence.

Agent Meyer decided to help ease the pressure off the mayor. "Listen, Ralph, only the CIA is aware of your involvement. We're willing to keep our mouth shut and roll with you on the whole Lucky conspiracy."

The mayor quickly snapped out of his daze. "How?"

"Oh, now you want to speak? You're not even going to answer my question, boss? You are going to answer me. Did you have the commissioner assassinated?"

The mayor finally looked up at his old friend. "Yes, I was the mastermind behind it."

"Are you fuckin' serious? I have kept my mouth shut on a lot of things, but you are alone on this one. You're not bringing me down on this one," Richard said as he was walking toward the door.

"Not so fast, Richard. We know you were not involved in the assassination, but you were involved in many other illegal activities. You can't leave. You are now involved in this situation, too," Agent Meyer said.

"What do you mean, I can't leave?"

"The CIA will not sit back and allow you to jeopardize this investigation. You already know too much. Please close the door and come back in. Don't make this hard on yourself or your family."

Richard was obviously shaken by the harsh words coming out of the agent's mouth. He closed the door and walked back over toward his boss like a little bitch with his tail tucked.

"Listen, Mr. Mayor, the CIA has handled all the major conspiracy and terrorist threats against the United States of America for over fifty years. There have been thousands of threats that never went public. They were kept under the radar for a reason. This current situation fits the under-the-radar file. We can't afford another major corruption case. If this information hits the press, we will have another riot, and this time many more will die."

"Sounds good to me. What do we have to do?"

"Not so fast, Mr. Mayor. You're not getting away so easy. There will be harsh penalties handed down to you, which will include your resignation."

"My what? That's unacceptable," the mayor quickly responded.

"Unfortunately, you don't have options. You are a disgrace to the United States government and its history. Please, don't think our services are to help you. We're here to keep the good faith of this country. The plan is to frame Lucky. In order for that to happen, you have to capture him. We need you to capture him as quick as possible, before he starts revealing evidence about the truth. Tomorrow morning I will have a team of analysts back here reviewing all your files on Lucky, his ex-partners, Commissioner Fratt, and the Coleman shooting. I expect your full cooperation in this entire investigation."

"So you expect me to just hand over information that will crucify all of us in court?" the mayor shot back.

"Again, our investigation will be silent. We just want to make sure we destroy all evidence. That way it doesn't resurface years later. We're protecting our end. We don't want our involvement to be known. Trust me, your resignation won't be a surprise to the city. Most of the people are calling for it, anyway. Just consider this an early retirement. But if you decide not to cooperate, then you will have to answer to your involvement in the assassination and possibly face life in prison. Your choice. I will give you sixty seconds to decide."

"I don't need any time, if you guarantee no jail time or public humiliation. Richard and I will fully cooperate," the mayor said. "So, Agent Meyer, what's the plan? What kind of support are we going to receive in framing Lucky?"

"Let's get one thing clear. We're not here to play your little cop-and-robber games. We are not capturing Lucky. Our job is to help frame the son of a bitch. We will provide national attention. We will feature him on *America's Most Wanted* tonight. That way we'll receive the audience we need. Lucky can't keep running around in other states so freely and not be recognized. Once you guys capture him, we will then start releasing different bogus footage of him at the crime scene. In order for it to work, we need him in custody first. Here is my business card. I will see you soon."

"Wait. What about me?" the mayor asked.

"If I was you, I would start rehearsing my resignation," Agent Meyer shot back as he walked out of the office.

"Excuse me, if I may. Elections are about eleven months away. Right now, this city is not ready to lose its mayor. I know some are calling for his resignation, but it will cause more damage than good. At least the mayor could finish his term. Can we work something out where he would just make it public that he won't run for a second term?" Richard begged for his boss's job, even after his betrayal.

"I will bring this information to my superiors. As long as you guys fully cooperate, I don't see why they won't agree," Agent Meyer said.

As soon as the agents left the room, and the mayor and Richard were finally alone, Richard didn't waste any time letting his boss know how he felt. "I'm extremely disappointed. How can you kill one of your best friends? You know what? Don't even answer that question. I have a lot of work to do before Agent Meyer gets upset. I will see you in the morning."

"Listen, Richard, I'm sorry I didn't tell you, but I had to do it. The commissioner fucked up by not taking care of Lucky right after the Coleman shooting. If he'd done his job, Lucky would have never shown up in court, and we wouldn't be in this situation we're in now."

"Fuck you! Agent Meyer was right. You are a disgrace to the U.S. government," Richard said as he left the office, slamming the door behind him.

After Richard left, Ralph Gulliano just sat there in complete silence, his whole life flashing right in front of him. He thought about his wife and kids and felt ashamed. He wasn't only raised better, but he took an oath to protect and serve. He was no different than any other common criminal. In fact, he was below a criminal. More like a scumbag, a worthless piece of shit. He was basically the top dog, so that made him a kingpin, but with legal and political powers.

Ralph kept picking up the phone and hanging up. He was scared to call his wife. He didn't even know how to begin. He couldn't just call her and say, "Hey, I killed Commissioner Fratt and I have to resign, but the good part is I don't have to go to jail." His wife wouldn't even know how to handle such a confession.

As the mayor sat in his office, trying to figure out a way to call his wife, the governor made his way in the office. The mayor was thrown off by his visit. He thought the governor knew about the CIA leaving his office.

"News travels fast, I see," the mayor said.

"What news?"

"So you don't know?"

"Do I know what?" the governor asked with a confused look.

That was when it hit the mayor. He realized that the governor's main connections were with the federal government, and he might not be aware about the CIA's involvement. He kept his mouth shut about the assassination, but he had to tell him something because now he was curious.

"Right before you left, Richard and I were talking about my future, and I decided not to run for reelection. I think the city needs a fresh start."

"I don't know. The way you handled the riot and restored order, you may get reelected. You are a hero. Don't let those small accusations scare you. Just take your time and think about it. Anyway, I'm here to see if you have any new leads on our prey."

"No new leads, but I do have great news. John Walsh from *America's Most Wanted* is doing a whole show on Lucky tonight."

"That's great news. I don't know why we waited to get on the show. We need all the national attention we can get. We need to make it a two-million-dollar reward."

"A two-million-dollar reward would make anyone talk." The mayor flashed his trademark smile. "But where are we going to get the money from?"

"I have connections. Plus, after the *America's Most Wanted* feature, it will be a lot easier to come up with the money."

They continued talking for the next forty-five minutes, forty of which were spent on Lucky. They both had not slept in days. Chasing Lucky had drained them and destroyed their personal lives.

Lucky was back in Haze's room, doing push-ups and sit-ups, working out in complete darkness. He was revisiting some of the old training he used to do right after his mother had died. He knew, once he stepped back in New York, he would face the fight of his life.

As Lucky sat there motionless, concentrating, Haze came in and interrupted his training. "Lucky, hurry up! You have to see this! You are on TV again!"

Lucky at first was upset but then understood why Haze had interrupted him. He ran into the living room, turned the volume up on the TV, and couldn't believe his eyes and ears. He was actually on *America's Most Wanted.*

"Good evening, America. My name is John Walsh. For years I have captured criminals, but tonight it will be a different show. Tonight, America, we need your help in capturing an ex-police officer from New York. His name is Donald Gibson, but he is known as Lucky. This ex-police officer is wanted for numerous crimes, which include murder and drug trafficking. He's also believed to be the main suspect in Commissioner Brandon Fratt's assassination. He's considered armed and dangerous, so if you have any information on the whereabouts of this fugitive, please contact 1-800-OUTLAWS.

"Lucky was last seen in Glen Burnie, Maryland, where he was almost captured, but he shot a police officer and escaped. Based on information from our sources, he's believed to still be in Maryland, but he

could be anywhere. If you have any information that could lead to his arrest, call the hotline. There's a two-million-dollar reward."

Haze jumped up and turned the TV off. "Yo, he said two million dollars. Fuck *America's Most Wanted!* Don't worry. I'm not a snitch. There's no need to watch this show. You just let me know when we're making our next move."

"You a real muthafucka, Haze. They don't build criminals like you. Today, snitching is like a new style."

"Ha! Ha! You are right. But that's why I barely have friends. I can't trust these cats out here today. Muthafuckas are cruddy out here."

"*Cruddy?*" Lucky asked, confused.

"That's some B-more shit. It means a foul, grimy-ass nigga. I grew up in Baltimore, over east. Let me tell you. Baltimore got some cruddy-ass dudes, especially in Park Heights and Cherry Hill."

"Ha! *Cruddy*. I never heard of that saying before. I heard of Cherry Hill before, though. I pulled over some Baltimore cats years ago. They were looking for Washington Heights but were lost in Spanish Harlem. They had like sixty thousand cash and three guns on them. We took everything, put them back on the highway, and sent them back down here."

"Y'all kept the dough and gats?"

"Hell yeah, we did. That was an easy come-up. That's how we carry it. I guess we were cruddy cops, you could say."

"Damn! I should have became a cop. I didn't know you could get paid like that."

Haze sparked another blunt, but Lucky passed on it. He wanted to stay focused, and the weed was only going to make him tired. All he wanted was to return to the room and continue working out.

"If you're not smoking anymore, then I'm not smoking. We have to stay focused. I feel you."

Again, Lucky was impressed with his dedication. He was a bit concerned that Haze might later change his mind and go after that two-million-dollar reward. He believed the young soldier was true to his word, but couldn't trust him 100 percent.

At the time, Lucky wasn't too concerned. He had major issues to worry about. Like, why Sergio still hadn't called him back. His phone was turned off, and all calls were going straight to voice mail. The frustration was building inside of Lucky, and it was making him second-guess himself about Sergio as well. Plus, he didn't like something Sergio had said to him in their last phone conversion earlier in the day. All he needed was Blood's phone number. He needed to get in contact with Blood as soon as possible. That way he'd know when he'd be heading up to New York. He felt safe in Haze's apartment, but he was eager to get back up there and find Diamond and his money.

Lucky wasn't about to let *America's Most Wanted* stop his flow. He needed another plan, one that would get him up to New York safely. He was going to give Sergio till the morning to call him back before acting on his own. With Captain Tuna and Speedy still in jail, Lucky knew the mayor was receiving federal help in capturing him, especially after the president's visit. That was the reason why he was waiting on Blood's number. He needed soldiers who were ready to kill. He knew Blood wouldn't turn him down and would do anything to avenge his brother's death. It was a fight he couldn't do all alone. He needed a team, but not just any regular squad. He wanted certified players with experience to play along with him.

That was when he thought about his best friend, Divine, the one person he could count on for anything. Their friendship was solid as a rock and went back to their high school days. They'd actually played football together and graduated in the same class. After high school, Lucky stayed home, while Divine went away to school in Philly. He lasted only a year in school before he was back on the block, hustling. Divine was the one who'd convinced Lucky to invest in the storage facility.

Lucky dropped a few more tears for his comrade and best friend. There was nothing like losing a loved one, but when they got killed in front of you, that memory would haunt you forever. Then he continued to work out, hoping it would help him stop thinking about his homie.

Chapter 6

Going Back to New York

Around two in the morning, Lucky's phone started ringing. Sergio had finally called him back.

"Damn, Sergio! I been trying to fuckin' call you all day. What's up with you?"

"I'm sorry. My girlfriend, she's crazy. She turned my cell phone off. She didn't want anyone to interrupt us."

"I'm over here hiding from the federal government, and you up there playing little sex games with your girl? I just ask for one little favor, just one. I need Blood's number, that's all."

"I have the number for—"

Lucky interrupted him. "Just give me the fuckin' number, Sergio."

After Lucky wrote the number down, he ended the call without notifying Sergio, making it known he was disappointed in him. Lucky dialed Blood's number, and it rang for about six times before he picked up.

"Who the fuck is this?" a grouchy, intoxicated Blood asked because it was so late.

"It's me."

Blood jumped off the couch. He knew who it was. He grabbed another phone off the coffee table and walked to his kitchen. "I'm going to call you right back," he said before ending the call. He called Lucky back from a prepaid cell phone.

Lucky picked up on the first ring.

"Hey, no need to say names. I know who this is. I've been waiting on your call. These rats burned and killed my brother and Divine. What's up? Where you at? They got the heat on you hard for killing the commissioner."

"I know. I'm still out of town, in Maryland. I need to get up there. For the record, I didn't shoot the commish. They're trying to pin that on me."

"Whatever you need, talk to me. You need help getting to me? I have a minivan with a secret compartment large enough to fit you in. You will get into New York safely. Just give me till about noon. Give me the address."

"Bet. It sounds good. I need about ten thousand when you come down."

"No problem. I will holla. One."

Lucky turned toward Haze, who was anxiously waiting for the plan. "We're leaving noon tomorrow," he said.

Haze started clapping his hands in excitement. It was the moment he'd been waiting for. "I'm going to start packing."

Lucky sat down and leaned his head back. He felt bad for Haze. The reason why he asked Blood for ten thousand was to leave it with Haze. Lucky couldn't risk that boy's life. He didn't care if Haze was ready to ride or die for him. He just couldn't risk it, especially if he didn't have to. Once he got in contact with Blood, Haze's services were no longer needed. Lucky decided not to inform Haze about the new decision. He didn't want him to get upset that he wasn't going and get any funny ideas about collecting the two million dollars.

As Haze packed, Lucky jumped in the shower. He decided to wash up and kill time. In the shower, all he thought about was Diamond. He was devastated and embarrassed by her lack of judgment. Lucky felt like he did what any other real man would have done. He set her free to live her life because his was already occupied. He didn't want to continue holding her back.

As the warm water was hitting his head, his emotions were getting the better of him. Right before tears came down his face, he snapped out of it and started thinking about their sex life. They'd had the wildest times. She used to give the best head, spitting on his dick and sucking it up, driving him crazy. She knew how to work it. She used to keep sucking until his knees buckled.

Lucky grabbed his dick, which was already hard like the sidewalk. He started jerking it slowly as he thought about those nights Diamond sucked him off. He only thought about those times when she swallowed him.

Usually when Lucky masturbated and thought about those times, it would only take a few minutes, sometimes seconds, for him to bust his nut. This time it was different. It was going over five minutes, and he was still jerking his meat. He even started beating at a fast pace and still no feelings. His dick was starting to get soft. He stopped and let the water continue to bounce off his head. He leaned against the wall, finally realizing Diamond was officially out of his life. He couldn't even jerk off thinking about her anymore. After his shower, he went straight to bed and called it a night.

As Lucky slept, the mayor received a call from Special Agent Jenkins, who was still down in Maryland.

"Good evening, sir, I have new intel, and I couldn't wait until the morning to call you."

"This better be good."

"Remember the suspect who died at the hospital? The one you guys mistakenly identified as Lucky?"

"I remember. His name was Dwayne Mooks. What's your point, agent? I'm about to hang up if you called me to talk about a dead suspect."

"Bear with me, sir. Dwayne Mooks is better known as Pee-Wee. He has a brother named Daquan Mooks, nickname Blood. These brothers as a team were vicious, and their rap sheet is unbelievable. We're on our way back to New York. We believe Lucky will get in contact with him. Blood always worked together with his brother. If Lucky knew Pee-Wee, I'm sure he knew Blood. We are going to stake out several of his hangouts and see what we come up with."

"That's great news. Keep me updated, and let me know if you need additional help once you arrive in New York." The mayor hung up the phone in excitement.

Things were going to get real interesting in the next few days in New York. Lucky and both special agents were heading to the same location. It was going to be another shoot-out similar to the night the storage facility was raided. New York was not in a position to handle another gun battle. Most of the city's cops were out in the streets, working with the community, building the city together as one.

By the time the sun started rising, Lucky was already on the floor, doing his exercise. After three hundred and fifty push-ups and two hundred sit-ups, he jumped back in the shower. When he came out, he saw Haze doing push-ups in the living room.

Lucky laughed to himself because little man was a rider for real. "I see you bustin' those push-ups out," he yelled.

Haze jumped up. "Shit! I'm trying to be like you. I just did eighty."

"Ha! Eighty? That ain't shit."

"How many you did?"

"A quick three-fifty. I usually do five hundred, but I'm a li'l out of shape."

"Three-fifty, for real? Damn! I need to get my weight up. We still have time before the ride gets here. I'm going to try to do at least two hundred."

Lucky just laughed as he walked away and went back in the room to take a quick nap. As he lay on the bed, he started thinking about Tasha. He knew she must be a nervous wreck. He had to call her. He already knew what she was going to say. Plus, he'd always feared Tamika would snatch the phone from her mother and ask him to come home. He just hoped one day they would understand and forgive him. He missed them so much. He couldn't wait to reunite with them. He made a promise to his little girl and wasn't about to let her down like he did in the past.

A few hours later, Lucky's phone started ringing.

"Yo."

"Hey, it's me. According to the GPS, we should be there in, like, ten minutes, my nigga."

"A'ight bet, I'm ready."

Lucky jumped up and threw his shirt on. Then he grabbed his gun and book bag. When he got out to the living room, Haze was waiting by the door.

"I heard the phone ring. What's up? When we are leaving?"

"Listen, Haze, sit down. We need to talk."

"Aw shit! That's what my father used to say to me all the time when he was about to break some bad news."

"It's not bad news. It's just some shit you don't want to hear. Listen, I can't bring you with me to New York. This is a suicide mission, li'l homie. This is a real war, a war that's beyond guns and money. I'm always going to keep it real. The chances of you coming back alive are slim to none."

"C'mon. What the fuck are you talking about? I know the risk."

"You are not listening. You are not going."

"I thought you said it wasn't bad news, 'cause right now I'm feeling like shit. You fucked my wet dream up."

"When my boy Blood gets here in a few minutes, he's going to come in with a bag filled with money, ten thousand to be exact. That's all for you, li'l homie."

"Get the fuck out of here! For real?"

"I told you I appreciate all you have done for me, and I'm going to need you to keep your mouth shut after I leave."

"You still questioning my heart. You never trusted anyone in your life? I'm not a snitch."

"I have in the past, but not lately. Money makes humans act like scavengers."

Right after Lucky finished speaking, his cell phone started ringing, and someone was knocking at the door. He walked toward the door, looked through the peephole, and saw Blood in a medical uniform. He opened the door and let him in.

"Blood, what the fuck you doing in a medical uniform? You are a funny muthafucka. I'm sure glad to see you, bro," Lucky said as he hugged him.

"I'm glad to see you, too. You ready? Let's hit the road. We'll talk on the road."

"Oh, I'm ready. Did you bring the money?"

"It's in the black bag." Blood handed him the bag.

Lucky passed the bag right over to Haze and told him, "I'm a man of my word. I'm going to miss you, li'l homie. I haven't met good youngblood in a long time. Stay focused and invest this money in something positive. Open up a store or something. I need one last favor. Call this number from a pay phone and let her know I'm okay and that I will be home soon."

"You got it." Haze walked up to him and hugged him. "Thanks for the life lessons. I paid attention to everything you said to me. I'm going to miss you, and,remember, you're always welcome back. Please, tell the mayor to kiss my ass right before you kill him."

"I got you. I will make sure I tell him to kiss your ass. Hey, you never know, I might be calling you to come up to New York."

"I'll be waiting."

Lucky grabbed his bag and went out the door with Blood. He was bugging when he read the sign on Blood's van—MEDICAL TRANSPORTATION SERVICES.

Blood turned to Lucky. "Who in the fuck was that, Lucky?" he asked.

"A street hustler I bumped into. I offered him money if I could stay at his house."

"Doesn't he know you have a two-million-dollar reward on your head? You took a big risk in trusting him."

"I didn't have any other choice. I took a chance on him, I know, but I had to. Little man is legit. I really do want to bring him with me."

"Then bring him. It's not like there isn't any room."

"Nah, it's better this way."

"Okay, here's the deal. You can ride in the backseat. My windows are tinted enough, so they won't see you."

"What you mean? That's it? I was just on *America's Most Wanted*, and you just want me to ride in the backseat because you have dark tints? I don't think so, bro."

"Ha! Nah, this minivan is equipped with two large refrigerators. I transport body parts, mainly hearts and kidneys. The larger fridge in the back is the secret compartment. You will be able to jump in there if we get pulled over. Once we get close to the George Washington Bridge, you'll have to get in until we get to Harlem."

"Sounds a lot better now. C'mon, let's roll out of here."

"What happened that night, Lucky?" Blood asked, speaking of the night his brother and best friend were murdered.

"Aw, man, I still remember it like it was yesterday. I pulled up to the storage and noticed police was already staking out the spot. I went inside, and your brother and Divine also seen the cops from the security camera. We got our big guns out, and we were ready. I went up to the roof with Divine, while Pee-Wee guarded the front door.

"By the time we reached the roof, there were over fifty cops pulling up and running up to the front door. We were shooting, Pee-Wee was shooting, and the cops were returning fire. Then, out of nowhere, a fuckin' sniper takes out Divine with a shot to the head right in front of me, my nigga. I saw the sniper's location and was able to take him out. As I ran back downstairs to reunite with your brother, there was fire and black smoke everywhere, so I couldn't go back downstairs."

"Damn! They burned my brother alive, those dirty-ass pigs. At least you walked away, but don't worry. We'll get our revenge."

As Blood was driving up I-95 North, Lucky felt like shit. He didn't come clean about leaving Pee-wee alone and bailing out on him. Lucky knew he couldn't come clean, because he needed Blood's help more than anything at the moment. Why ruin it by coming clean? Maybe one day he would tell Blood the truth, but not in this lifetime.

Lucky decided to ask Blood about the body-part gig, to get his mind off things. "So, what's good with this body-part shit? How you into this business? You caught me off guard with this genius move. I never heard of anything as slick as this."

"I got this idea from this bitch I used to fuck with in Atlanta. She told me her father ran his own business for twenty-five years. He actually helped me get all my licenses and permits. This is the slickest shit ever, Lucky. I even get special treatment if I get pulled over by police. They usually let me go. You can't hold up a heart or a lung from surgery when there are people dying."

"Ha! Damn, Blood! This here is a gold mine."

"Who are you telling? This minivan could hold up to twenty bricks of cocaine and about ten pounds of weed. I'm about to get about three more of these bad boys and just take over I-Ninety-five. If you want in, let me know. I got you."

"Oh, I want in, but first I need to get back in the storage facility. I still have a lot of money in the stash room that's fireproof. I know my money is safe."

"Just let me know the plan. I'm down, just as long as we kill a few cops in the process. I'm not worried about money. I got plenty of it."

"It's not about just killing cops," Lucky quickly said, to get the idea out of his head.

"Maybe it's not, but I'm killing cops."

"I have a bigger plan. We're going after the big boy. The mayor."

"You want to kill the mayor? Damn, Lucky! I know I said let's go hard, but killing the mayor is extra hard. Didn't you already kill the commissioner?"

"I keep telling people I didn't pull the trigger. I didn't kill that pig. I wish I did. But don't forget, Blood, the mayor is the one responsible for your brother's death. We just can't let him get away with it. Trust me, I will work on a plan once we get back to New York. First,

I have to find that bitch Diamond. She's the one who dropped dime on us."

"Diamond? She was your bottom bitch. What happened? You see, that's why you can't bring bitches into the game. They get all emotional and personal."

"You don't have to tell me. I'm living proof that theory is true."

As they drove up in the middle of the afternoon, Lucky let his mind wander. He'd never worked alone with Blood before and was a little skeptical. Having a new partner made him think the job was too big for them to handle. In the back of his head, he knew it was going to be hard to kill the mayor. The whole ride up to New York, he kept trying to replay the morning Commissioner Fratt was assassinated. He couldn't understand why his memory was blurry. It was killing him not knowing what happened that morning. He was upset at himself for being weak and losing the battle with addiction.

If he hadn't snorted all that cocaine, he wouldn't have been in this cloud of darkness. He knew in his heart that he didn't pull the trigger. He wasn't equipped with the right type of weapon. In fact, Lucky thought maybe the mayor was the mastermind behind the hit. He didn't have proof, but he could try to make him confess, which would be almost impossible.

The long, quiet drive was making Lucky doze off.

About three hours later, Blood tapped him on his leg. "Wake up, son. I need you to get in the fridge. We coming up on the George Washington Bridge. And, don't worry. You'll be able to breathe in there."

"A'ight, but head to the Bronx first. I want to visit Sergio real quick. I need to ask him a few questions."

"A'ight. I'll jump on the Cross Bronx Expressway. Once we clear, I'll let you know. Don't close the fridge door all the way unless I ask you to."

Lucky went in the fridge and couldn't believe how easily he was able to fit in there. He was only in there for like twenty minutes before Blood called him out the box.

As they headed toward Sergio's house, Blood asked, "How come we need to visit Sergio?"

"Something he said over the phone just stuck in the back of my head, and I need to clarify it."

Blood quickly picked up on Lucky's vibe. "Oh, so this won't be a friendly visit. Damn! Is everybody snitching now? That's the new hustle, I see."

"I don't know if he's snitching, but my hand will be on my gun when I go in his apartment."

As they got near Sergio's building, Lucky asked him to park up the block and watch the building for a few. As they sat there, two suits came out of the building.

"You see that shit, Lucky? They look like homicide."

"Nah, they're either the feds or the CIA. Those are thousand-dollar suits they're wearing."

"You think they just came from out of your boy's crib?" Blood asked.

"I don't know, but we about to find out. Let's wait a minute or two before we go upstairs."

They sat there and only waited about thirty seconds. Lucky was eager to find out what was going on. They slowly crossed the street, and when they reached the building, they ran upstairs to Sergio's door and rang his bell.

Sergio looked through the peephole and saw it was Lucky. He wondered if Lucky had seen the agents leave his building. He couldn't see Blood, who was leaning against the wall, out of sight, waiting for the door to unlock.

Sergio was hesitant to open the door, but Lucky's knocks kept getting louder. When he finally unlocked the door, both Lucky and Blood forced their way in.

Lucky jumped on top of him and put his gun right in his mouth. “Explain why the feds just left your apartment, muthafucka.”

Sergio couldn’t speak, because the barrel was down his throat. He was choking, and spit was coming out his mouth. When Lucky removed the gun from his throat, Sergio began to cry, saying, “Please, let me explain. I will never snitch. That wasn’t the feds. It was the CIA. They approached me. You have to believe me, man. Please don’t kill me.”

As soon as Lucky heard *the CIA*, he picked up Sergio and threw him on the sofa.

“Let me shoot this piece of shit, Lucky!” Blood yelled as he cocked back his gun. “He’s already crying like a bitch. Let me shoot him.”

“Chill. Not yet, Blood,” Lucky said, pushing him away. “Let him talk first. Maybe, just maybe, he can save his own life. So, Sergio, please tell us what they wanted.”

Sergio looked around his living room before answering. He was looking around for some type of weapon, and trying to think of a way to escape. After not seeing anything, he realized his only chance of staying alive was to tell Lucky the truth.

“They came in here looking for you. I don’t know how they knew, I swear to God, and I didn’t tell anyone. Those muthafuckas just showed up at my door. They’re blaming you for the assassination. They kept mentioning some conspiracy theory shit. I don’t know. They just want my help.”

Lucky backhanded him across his mouth and grabbed him by his hair with his right hand. He pulled his head back, placed his gun on his lips, and looked in his eyes. “Stop bullshittin’! What kind of help?”

"They want me to call them next time I hear from you. They offered me five hundred thousand dollars to testify that you were the shooter. They want me to frame you for the assassination." Sergio wiped the blood that was dripping from his mouth.

"It doesn't make sense. I know the CIA has ways of locating individuals, but how in the fuck did they track you down? is the question. Something is missing. Your story sounds funny."

"That's because he's lying," Blood yelled. "Slap that bitch-ass nigga again, or let me do it."

Lucky, still holding Sergio by his hair, pushed the barrel in his mouth. "Listen carefully to the next question. Your answer will determine your fate. When we were on the phone, you mentioned the one hundred thousand I gave Diamond. No one knew how much money I gave her, except Diamond and Divine. Divine is dead, so how in the fuck you know about the money?"

Sergio once again attempted to lie. "I remember one time you said—"

Lucky moved the gun around in his mouth. "C'mon now, Sergio, you know better than that. I never reveal info about my plans. How did you know? This will be my last time asking. I'm not playing," Lucky said as he placed his index finger on the trigger.

"Okay, okay. Diamond never left New York. She didn't want to live in Maryland. She knew you were never coming back. She was devastated. I let her stay here a few days before she went back home. She never told me where home was, but that's how I know about the money. I'm sorry I never told you."

Lucky let Sergio go, took a few steps back, and just stared at him. He wanted to empty his whole clip in his face, but he needed more answers because now it was getting deep. Those missing pieces were coming to life.

He paced Sergio's living room back and forth, thinking about the bomb Sergio had just dropped. It really left him at a loss for words, but it gave him a lot to think about.

"Last time I was here, you left to visit a female friend. Were you talking about Diamond?"

"Hell fuckin' no. I would never touch Diamond. She slept right on the couch. She didn't have anywhere else to go, and she didn't want to stay in a hotel with all that money. After she left, I never heard from her again, I swear," Sergio said, pleading for his life. "Please, believe me."

"I'm still not convinced. If she was here, you must have known about her dropping a dime on me. You didn't stop her. Oh, now I fucking get it. She either called the cops from here or your cell phone. That's why the fuckin' CIA was here, right? They traced the call."

Lucky grabbed Sergio by his hair again and threw him back on the floor. "Blood, go in his bedroom and grab a few pillows. This bitch is dead."

"No, wait. C'mon, Lucky, you were like a father to me. I looked up to you."

"I'm glad you understand why I have to kill you. You violated the code. I also looked at you as my son. I'm going to punish you like our ancestors punished their kids when they betrayed the family. Capital punishment."

Lucky used Sergio's belt to tie his hands behind his back and turned the volume on the radio up high. Blood came back with three pillows. Lucky placed one over each of Sergio's kneecaps and told Blood to hold one over his face.

Sergio began screaming, hoping one of his neighbors would hear him and call 9-1-1. "Help, please help!" he screamed.

"Shut the fuck up, bitch! Apply more pressure, Blood! Keep him quiet!" Lucky said as he pointed his gun at Sergio's knees and shot both of them.

The pillows actually worked, muffling the sound of the gunshots. Plus, with hip-hop blasting through the speakers, Sergio's neighbors were unaware that he was getting tortured to death.

As he lay there screaming, losing consciousness, and damn near bleeding to death, Lucky decided to give him one last chance to come clean.

"Blood, move the pillow away from his face," Lucky said as he leaned over. He pointed his bloody gun at Sergio and said, "This is your last chance to save your own ass. Where did Diamond go? And is the CIA on their way to meet her?"

Sergio was coughing blood, trying to catch his breath. "All I know, she said she was going back home, and that was it. The CIA didn't ask about her. They asked about your daughter."

Lucky quickly got worried, because the CIA knew how to find their prey. "Everyone is looking for my daughter," he said, trying to play it off. He didn't want to show Sergio he was concerned. "Is there anything else you want to add? Because, right now, I'm thinking you don't care about your life too much. You're not giving me anything to work with." He'd just about had it with Sergio.

"I guess I'm not such a good criminal, after all. Maybe I needed better training. You never—"

Lucky grabbed the pillow from Blood, put it over his face, and shot him twice. He wasn't about to allow Sergio to disrespect him. He was the one who'd crossed the line.

Sergio did mess Lucky's head up with the new twist. Now his family wasn't safe down in Atlanta. Sergio could have told them they were down there.

Lucky was mad that he'd killed him before asking him. He got caught in the moment and acted off his reflex. With a gun in his hand and his mind set on using it, the power of holding the weapon manipulated his thought process and made him pull the trigger. Caught in the moment, he forgot all about using patience in his approach. He had wanted to kill Sergio within the first ten seconds of entering the apartment and was surprised he'd waited as long as he did. At least he had confirmation that Diamond indeed was the one who leaked the info and called the cops.

Lucky made a living out of reading people's eyes, and he honestly couldn't tell if Sergio was lying. But he sounded believable. The only way to be sure was to find Diamond and get her to explain herself. He still didn't know where she was located. She could either be back home, like Sergio stated, or she was under protective custody. One way or the other, he was going to find her.

But now he had a new concern. His family down in Atlanta might be in danger. He was going to have to call Tasha himself. He couldn't send anyone else. He needed to speak to her directly and explain the situation. The call was not going to be an easy one. Tasha could very well tell him to fuck off, or she could ride, like he was hoping.

Lucky was glad he was back in New York, where he had connections. Down in Maryland, he was a sitting duck in unfamiliar territory.

After Lucky and Blood wiped down whatever furniture they might have touched, they left Sergio's apartment. Blood wanted to know where Lucky wanted to go next.

Lucky said, "I need a hotel room to lay low for a few days."

"A hotel room, never. You could stay with me, Lucky."

"Nah. I already lost two good friends because of my past. I don't want to have to lose you, too. A hotel room is all I need."

"A'ight, but around here all we have is fuck motels. I know you don't want to stay in one of those nasty places. I can't allow that."

"Ha! I feel you. I can't stay in New Jersey. I'm not trying to cross any tolls."

"Look, I got this bad bitch that's out of town, in Atlanta, for a few weeks, handling business. I got the keys to the apartment, which is my personal stash house. You could stay there if you want. No one knows about the place."

"Where she live?"

"She's right in Harlem, right off Riverside Drive, on 168th Street. It's a three-bedroom condo. You'll have it all by yourself. Plus, it has its own security camera system. I know you love the sound of that."

"For real, or are you bullshitting me?"

"For real, fam. This is where I keep my money and most of my product. I have to keep an eye on things. I paid like twenty thousand for the alarm, and I have a few computers as well. You'll have all the technology you need to keep you busy while we find this bitch. Are we still going after the mayor or what?"

"Hell yeah, we are. The apartment sounds perfect."

Lucky thought the apartment idea was great. He would get a chance to hide and relax a bit until he came up with his next plan. He was glad to hear about the security setup.

Blood drove him straight to the apartment, and they went in unseen. Blood showed him how to work the security system, and he showed Lucky where he kept his guns, which included two AK-47s, at least twelve different handguns, and what looked like a few pipe bombs.

"Are those bombs, Blood?"

"Listen, after my brother was murdered, I was going to run up in city hall and blow a few muthafuckas up. My peoples talked me out of it, so now I'm looking for one of these Hala muthafuckas."

"I don't understand, Blood. Why are you looking for an Arab?"

"So I can sell this shit to him. I don't need them anymore. They might strap them on themselves and run up in city hall."

Lucky couldn't stop laughing. "You are one crazy cat."

"Shit! Them Halas kill themselves all the time. I'm sure if I offered them six figures, they will do it. I'm dead serious, too."

"Like I said, you are loony, but those bombs could come in handy."

"I'm ready when you ready. They're not getting away with killing my brother. I have to bounce and take care of business. Don't worry. No one should show up here, so if anybody rings the bell, you know what to do."

"Oh, trust me, I will be up and ready. I won't get caught with my dick in the dirt." Lucky grabbed his private parts.

"Here, take this phone. My number is the only one saved on it. Call this number if you need anything. I'll come back later and bring you food. You'll be good here. I love you, and I'm glad you called."

"Don't worry about bringing food. I'll handle it. Just give me a few days. Then come through. Be careful out there. Remember, we have all kind of alphabet boys after us."

"I feel you. I'm not trying to get caught with my dick in the dirt, either. I'll just call you."

After Blood left, Lucky sat on the plush leather sofa and watched the fifty-inch plasma. He was trying to get his mind off all the drama that took place no more than thirty minutes ago. He wanted to catch up on some of the current news about him. In Maryland, the news channels spoke about him briefly and did bullshit stories on him. In New York it was a different story. Lucky was on TV more than the O.J. trial.

When he turned the TV on, he just caught the end of Destine Diaz's report about the latest on the Coleman trial, and about Captain Tuna and Speedy still being in Central Booking for their own protection, instead of being transferred to Rikers Island. Lucky laughed when he heard about his former partners still in the lockup and with no bail. He knew support for them was no longer existent. He only wished they were a lot easier to reach. Being locked in protective custody was their life support. Once they came out, they were as good as dead. It didn't matter if they were home or up north, serving a bid.

As Lucky finished watching the news, he got ready to jump in the shower. Before turning the TV off, he said to himself, "I need to set up an exclusive with Destine Diaz."

Lucky knew that would be impossible. The only way that could happen was if he kidnapped her and forced her to interview him. He doubted she would accept his invitation without warning the cops, or at least he wasn't going to take that chance. He figured the interview would allow him to give his side of the story, and so the public might take it a bit easier on his character. He wasn't going to try to fool the public and lie. He was going to admit his guilt. He just wanted to make sure he cleared his name on certain charges, since the media and government made him look like a monster. For Lucky, it was very important to him the way he was remembered. He just wanted to remind all New Yorkers and Americans that corruption still existed and was acceptable across corporate America.

Chapter 7

117th Street and Seventh Avenue

After a forty-five-minute shower, all Lucky could think about was Sergio's last words. The CIA was now looking for his daughter. But he also couldn't stop thinking about Diamond. He believed she was still in New York and was plotting with Sergio to get his money. They both were money-hungry snakes.

He had two plans. One was to set up an interview with Destine Diaz; the other was to locate Diamond. If she was hiding in her hometown, Little Rock, Arkansas, it was going to be a challenge. If she was still in New York, then it was going to be easy to capture her.

Lucky didn't waste time in working on his blueprints. He logged on the Internet and into his private e-mail account. He needed to get in contact with a few of his old connects. He sent an e-mail to his Department of Motor Vehicle's connect, Asia, with Diamond's real name, Tracey Sanders, and her hometown. Asia, reliable as a bulletproof vest, would get back to Lucky within twenty-four hours. Asia didn't know Lucky's true identity. They'd met on a Web site called MyPlace.com. Asia ran her own private investigation business. Lucky conducted all his business through her Web site and communicated only via e-mail. After he sent her the e-mail, he logged off the Internet, turned the computer off, and unplugged it. He was covering his tracks, just in case the CIA or the feds were spying on Asia's company.

Lucky was paranoid. He plugged the computer back in and waited as it booted up. As he waited, he turned his attention back to the TV when he heard the Colemans were having another press conference. He jumped off his seat, got closer, and turned the volume up.

Laura was at the front stage like the strong black woman she was.

"Good evening. We decided to call this press conference because we wanted to update and address certain issues concerning our situation. I remember last time I held a press conference at my front door, we were shut down. The TVs went blank. Just in case that happens this time around, you could log on to our Web site, Perrycoleman.org. We are streaming live, and you will be able to see the entire press conference.

"Okay, let's get back to the serious matter at hand.

"I know New Yorkers have suffered enough, and right now, most are only concerned with the recovery process after the riots. I just want to bring closure and also begin my own personal healing and rebuilding process.

"I have met with the district attorney, and they have confirmed that both police officers who are in lockup have agreed on a plea deal. Each officer will face manslaughter one charges and will be sentenced to nine years to life. I couldn't believe the district attorney offered this deal without our approval. I would have loved to see the charges remain at murder one and they each get twenty-five to life for killing my son. We are bitter, but the district attorney has also made us aware of the numerous charges still pend-

ing against the dirty cops. They are still facing life in prison, which I hope they get. I'm just happy to hear that the trial is over, and they will at least serve nine years and spend the rest of their lives on parole.

"We, as a family, just want to turn the page on this book. I want to thank New York for all their support during these hard times. The city already has contacted our lawyers about a settlement before the civil trial begins. I want to go public and say, I promise to donate twenty percent of our settlement to the city. We want to help rebuild this great city.

"I also want to send a personal message to Donald 'Lucky' Gibson. Thank you. Thank you for coming forward and telling the truth. Thank you for the help. And I know in my heart you are not behind the assassination. Lucky, if you are listening, thank you. When the smoke clears, everyone will see that because of your bravery, we have won the battle with corruption. You sacrificed your own life to save others and rebuild the truth. I understand you were not a saint and you have done your share of dirt, but I just want to let you know that in our household you are considered a hero, a misunderstood one, but a hero. Thank you."

As soon as Mrs. Coleman finished speaking, her husband grabbed her by her hand, and they both walked in their house. In their minds, they were hoping it would be the last time they had to face the media.

Lucky was touched by her words and admired Mrs. Coleman's courage. "This old lady has balls," he said to himself. He was happy to hear that a settlement was already in the works. He knew the city was going to have to break the bank to satisfy the Colemans.

He was shocked to hear about the plea deal. He thought the nine years to life sentence was another sign that Tuna and Speedy were on their own. The city had stopped supporting them.

Lucky walked back over to the computer and logged back into his e-mail account. He sent another e-mail. He wanted more info on the mayor's whole operation. He wanted to know exactly which agencies were involved and how many special agents were in the streets, looking for him.

He needed to tap into the mayor's personal files and e-mail accounts. There was only one hacker capable of pulling off such a task. His name was Cyber Chris. He specialized in hacking into top-secret government files. Lucky had saved his ass thousands of times in the past. Because of Lucky's old ways, instead of arresting Cyber, he put him on his payroll.

Lucky sent him an e-mail with the information he needed and a thirty-thousand-dollar promise of pay. Lucky's credit was good, so Cyber wouldn't hesitate to accept the job. Lucky again logged out, shut down the computer, and unplugged it.

It was going on eight o'clock, and Lucky was hungry. He found a Domino's coupon and called to place an order for delivery. After eating a large pie and drinking almost a two-liter soda, he became sleepy and went straight to bed. He figured that eating that kind of meal would enable him to sleep through the night and first part of the morning. Once he got up the next day, he would log on and see if he received any replies from his two contacts.

Around midnight, the phone Blood left Lucky started ringing. It rang about six times before it finally woke Lucky out of his sleep.

"Hello," a hoarse Lucky said.

"Wake up. It's Blood. We have a problem."

"What's wrong?" Lucky asked as he jumped off the bed and started getting dressed.

"I think the feds are onto us. My boys said they're watching two of my spots."

"What? Are you sure they not those suits from Sergio's apartment?"

"The CIA? I don't think so. Plus, from what we know, they in regular clothes. One van is parked on 147th Street and a Crown Vic on 117th Street. There's only a driver in the van, but in the Crown Vic, there are two pigs sitting inside. We are making our move and taking all three of them out. You are safe in the apartment, so just stay there. I will call you when it's done."

"Let me ask you this. Have you noticed this kind of heat before?"

"No. Why?" a curious Blood asked.

"Then that means they know I'm in New York and that we are together. Anyone else in the crew know about you driving down to Maryland to pick me up?"

"I see where you heading. Only two people knew, and I trust them with my life. In fact, I trust them more than I trust you, real talk."

"I feel you, but I'm just saying, look at all the facts. Now that I'm back in town, the feds are watching you. Sergio didn't know I was on my way back up to New York. Maybe they know who your brother was." Lucky tried to throw off Blood and defuse what could've turned into an argument.

"Maybe, but the block is hot. After I handle these pigs, I'm going to lay low for a few days myself. I'm going to see my white bitch in Long Island."

After Lucky got off the phone with Blood, he couldn't sleep. He was half dressed, and his heart was still beating at a fast pace. He was ready for war, but if Blood told him he was safe and not needed, he was going to keep his black ass in that apartment.

Lucky still couldn't calm down. He wanted to drive to 117th Street and jump out with two guns in his hands. A nervous wreck, he was ready to set it off.

He was in the same state of mind he was in when he was a dirty cop. He didn't care about anyone, and less about his own life. His daughter didn't even come to mind. He was too selfish. Once he set his mind on a target, it was like going undercover. He blocked out the real world. The fantasy life became a reality role.

Lucky was feeling indestructible, but a little overwhelmed. With all the alphabet boys on his ass, his chances of surviving were slim. He couldn't keep killing everybody and surviving at the end like Rambo. His luck would run out one day.

He knew his fate. The problem was, he didn't care. He knew that if he stayed and continued the war, he was left with two options, dying or going to jail for life. And jail wasn't an option for him. In other words, he was ready to die.

He took his clothes off and just lay on the bed. He was trying to calm down and go back to sleep, but he couldn't. He figured he'd start working on how to set up the interview with Destine. Getting her number and address was going to be easy. How to approach her was going to be the hard part. He didn't know if he should show up at her job or at her home.

While Lucky thought about his next move, Blood was right on his FBI theory. Special agent's Marquis Jenkins and Angel Mendez were both parked across the street from one of Blood's operations on 117th Street and Seventh Avenue. They hadn't seen Blood or Lucky, but they felt like they were getting close.

"Marquis, you should call the mayor and give him an update."

"Chill, Angel. We don't have to call him every minute of the day. We are here under direct orders from the president. Fuck the mayor! Besides, I don't think he likes the fact we are on the case."

"I still think we should call him. He's still the mayor."

"Let's just wait until we have more proof. Right now we don't have shit, so why call?"

"Cool. Let's check in with Lee and see if anything changed on 147th Street."

"Lee, come in," Marquis radioed in.

"Everything is still quiet," Lee radioed back.

Marquis looked at his partner, and they both were on the same page. They knew something was off.

"Hey, when have you ever heard of these two streets being quiet? Maybe 117th Street, but not 147th Street. They must be on to us and shut shit down," Marquis said.

"Or maybe it's a setup," Angel added in a nervous tone.

"Setup? These muthafuckas don't have the balls to pull hits on cops. I worked in D.C. all my life, and for years it was known as the murder capital state. D.C. is no bigger than twenty miles. I survived the streets of Southeast. I know real killers. These fools are not killers."

"*Papi*, this is not D.C. I grew up in these streets. In New York they will smoke cops faster than crack. Either call for backup, or let's get the fuck out of here. Radio Lee and tell him to bounce as well," Angel said.

Marquis was a bit too cocky and ignored his partner's concerns. Being an ex-Navy SEAL and protecting the president, fear was never an issue for him. As they sat there, a car was coming down the street with the lights off. Marquis picked up on it quick and tapped his partner.

"Angel, it's time. Get ready. A car is creeping with their lights off. Unlock and crack your door. We may have to jump out that way," Marquis said as he cocked back his gun.

"About time we see some action. My Puerto Rican ass was getting tired. I'm up and ready," Angel said as he also cocked back his gun.

The car crept up and stopped right next to their car. The only reason Marquis didn't open fire was because he noticed the car was a Crown Victoria just like theirs, which was usually a cop car.

Good thing they didn't open fire. It was two narcotics detectives making their rounds. They rolled their window down, and Marquis did the same.

"To what do we owe the pleasure of having you guys snooping around in our turf? I'm Detective Marquis, and this is my partner, Detective Gomez. And you guys are?"

"I'm Detective Johnson, and that's my partner, Detective Simmons. We from the Thirty-third. This is our turf. You need permission to snoop in our block."

"We are working on a special assignment under direct orders from the mayor and president. Please continue driving down before you blow our cover," Marquis shot back.

"Oh, so you think the mayor has ranks out in these streets? I'm going to need some identification, since you are a smart-ass," Detective Johnson said as he stepped out of his car, his badge hanging down from his neck.

"All of this is not necessary. Fuck with us, and you will be on desk duty for the rest of your career!" Marquis said.

When Detective Johnson got out of the car to check for their identification, Marquis attempted to exit his car as well, but Johnson closed his door with his left hand, leaned over, whipped out his gun with his right, and emptied his clip inside of the car. Johnson didn't have time to look and see if they were wearing a vest, so he just aimed straight for their faces, shooting Marquis at least seven times, and hitting Angel at least four times.

Angel was able to let off a shot, but he ended up shooting his partner in the side of his stomach.

They were ambushed, caught off guard by Blood's crew posing as undercover cops. The trap worked, and they used the same tactic on Special Agent Lee Chang.

Blood's crew just finished pulling off three more hits on federal agents, two of whom worked directly under the president. The city didn't need more bad attention, especially the killing of more police officers. It was going to be a rude awakening for most in the morning.

Lucky was anxious in the apartment, not knowing what was going down. He knew Blood was a killing machine. He didn't care who or where he was dedicated to thuggin'.

It was going on six in the morning, and Lucky was working on about three hours of sleep. The first thing he did was turn on the TV and watch the news. As he sat there, his worst nightmare came true as the news anchor reported.

"Again, three federal agents were killed in Harlem. We will be right back with more details."

Lucky was frozen still. He just sat there motionless and didn't blink. He was hoping what he just heard was still a bad nightmare. He was so tired, he thought maybe he was hallucinating. He started pinching himself. He didn't move from the sofa and waited for the news to come back on.

Lucky already knew Blood was responsible for the killings and was more concerned with the identity of the federal agents. He wanted to know their names and their ranks. When the news came back on, he finally moved his body, sitting up and listening.

"We are back. I'm John Silverman. Three federal agents were gunned down in Harlem. We have Destine Diaz with the latest. Destine."

"Thank you, John, and yes, you are correct. Today, around three in the morning, three federal agents were killed in Harlem. Two were killed on 117th Street and one on 147th Street in Harlem. The information we are receiving is very conflicting. According to the police spokesperson, it seemed like an ambush, but one witness told a different story.

"We have a witness who claims she saw the shooting out her window and that the shooter had a police badge around his neck. The police department has rejected those accusations, claiming that many professional killers are now posing as police officers. That matter is still under investigation.

"So far the identity of only one of the agents has been revealed. He is Special Agent Lee Chang. He was killed on 147th Street, shot three times in the face at point-blank range. The other agents, who are being labeled John Doe number one and number two, were

also shot multiple times in the face. Again, the police department isn't saying much, except they still have no suspects, and they are not ruling out Lucky's involvement in the shooting.

"A source has stated that the agents were following leads on capturing Lucky. We will release more information as we receive it. The police are also asking anyone with information to please come forward. They are not letting us get close to the shooting scene here on 117th Street, but I will say this. There are a lot of suits down here. I'm assuming these two officers were of high rank or well loved. This is Destine Diaz reporting live from Harlem, Channel Five News."

Lucky didn't know how to feel. He was a little shocked to hear Blood had pulled off such a brazen move. The attack was too early, but you couldn't stop a man from getting his revenge. Blood's mind was made up, and no one could change it. The loss of his brother took him over the edge. He was ready to join him in the grave, but not without taking a few cops with him.

Lucky did love the slick move he pulled off, posing as police officers. He was sure the public was going to feel like the corruption in New York City would never end. With the past accusations against the city, many New Yorkers wouldn't be shocked to learn that cops were behind the killings.

Lucky didn't like that Destine mentioned his name in a negative way. He wasn't surprised, but he was bothered. Destine's tone and body language gave the impression that he was indeed involved in the shooting.

Lucky's cell phone started ringing. He knew it was Blood.

"You are one crazy muthafucka," he said. "You must have a death wish," Lucky said.

"I told you, once those pigs killed my brother and burned him, they created a monster. Anyway, I'm going away for a bit. Keep this cell with you, and I will keep in contact. But I will be off the phones for a while. The combination to the safe is 012449. That's my mother's date of birth. I have over two hundred thousand in there. You already know where all the guns are located. You do what you have to do. I will catch up with you later."

"Hold on, Blood. You sound like you're never coming back. What about your turf and transporting business?"

"Hey, I might not come back at all. I already shut down three locations. The heat is coming, so I'm out before I get burned. I'm not caring about any businesses right now, you feel me? If I was you, I wouldn't leave that apartment. You are safe as long as you don't show your face. Don't worry about my girl showing up. I will call her and make sure she stays in Atlanta a few more weeks."

"You take care and stay alive. They will hunt you down till they find you, and they will shoot to kill. Two of those agents were high-ranked agents. For now, I'm staying in here until I'm ready to go find Diamond, and then I'm bouncing back with baby moms. Take care, fam. You are the realest nigga I have ever known. Be easy." Lucky hung up the phone.

Lucky was still distressed. The whole situation was moving too fast for him. He still didn't know if Blood's move helped or hurt him. It was in his favor that Blood's crew posed as police officers. Though Lucky didn't like the rampage Blood was currently on, it was going to help his case. Once the FBI figured out Blood's motives and involvement, some of the heat would shift his way. Then maybe, just maybe, Lucky could clear his name. A lot of the accusations were not warranted. And though he wasn't expecting to be pardoned for his ways, he wasn't trying to be remembered as an animal.

Lucky went into the back room and cracked the safe open. Blood wasn't lying. The safe was filled with money. After counting it, he was shocked that it came to two hundred thousand and ten dollars. Lucky felt like he was back on top of the world. He had access to money, guns, and a computer. "I'm back, baby," he said to himself.

Lucky logged on the Internet to check his e-mails to see if his connects replied. Both Asia and Cyber Chris had replied. He opened Asia's e-mail first. She had great information, giving Lucky a current address for Diamond's mother, and another address for one of Diamond's sisters. He knew he could count on Asia.

Then he opened Cyber's e-mail. He promised to start working on it ASAP and to e-mail information before the day was up.

Lucky was happy that the momentum was finally starting to swing back his way. Down and out since the night the storage got raided, he had forgot the feeling of living on top. Once he opened the safe, that feeling came right back. When a man had complete power, such as money, guns, and balls the size of King Kong, the feeling was indescribable. The sky was the limit.

But Lucky was celebrating a little too early. He thought he had all he wanted, but in fact, he needed an extra body, someone who could move around town for him. With Blood out of state, he had no one else he could trust. He called up his little man from Maryland.

"Who is this?" Haze asked.

"What's good, little man?"

"Is this who I think it is?" Haze asked, a smile on his face.

"Yeah, it's me. Come to find out, I still need you up here with me. Do you still want to roll?"

"Hell yeah. I still have most of the money you left me. I will just bring it with me."

"Aw, man, that money is yours to keep. I don't want it back."

"No problem. I just need an address, and I'm on my way."

"Once you are in New York, just call this number, and I will have an address for you."

"You want me to come to Harlem?"

"Yeah, once you in Harlem, call me."

"Bet. I know how to get to 145th Street and Lenox Avenue."

"Perfect. Just call me."

After Lucky hung up the phone with Haze, he immediately started working on the plan. He wanted to drive to Arkansas himself, but he couldn't risk it. He was going to send Haze first and have him check both addresses. If he spotted Diamond, then he would head out there. He had a few pictures of Diamond in his e-mail and was going to print them and have them ready for Haze.

He started plotting his kidnap move. He had Destine's home address, so he was going to start off by staking out her house. He kept the TV on Channel 5, to keep up with any new updates.

The mayor was at the crime scene on 117th Street, walking around, shaking his head back and forth. He was speechless. Good thing he had Richard with him to serve as his mouthpiece and handle the press, since he was running out of excuses.

What the mayor was really scared of was a phone call from the president, who had two top agents killed, and he didn't have any answers or suspects. As Richard was gathering all the information, the mayor got on the phone, called his secretary, and asked to get in touch with the secretary of defense, Hilda Canton.

When the mayor got off the phone with his secretary, Richard was approaching. "What's the latest?" the mayor asked. "And please tell me Lucky was behind this."

"Well, Lucky's name, so far, has not come up. All the details are still sketchy, but according to a few witnesses, the shooter had a police badge around his neck. We doubt they were real police officers. So far, no leads."

"I can't believe we don't have any leads. Three federal agents are dead and we have no suspects, not even one clue? We are doomed. The press is going to have a field day with this bullshit."

"I will go handle the press. You, in the meantime, have other issues. Don't turn around, but the governor is heading this way, and boy, he doesn't look happy."

"God must hate me. He really does." The mayor waited to hear the governor's voice before he turned around.

"Ralph! Ralph, what in the hell happened here?"

"I'm still trying to figure it out myself," the mayor replied.

"Did you approve this operation?" he asked angrily.

"Listen, the president gave the two agents the green light to find Lucky. They didn't need my permission. They called me and said they were going to watch Pee-Wee's brother's several locations, and I said no problem, as long as they keep me updated."

"Who is Pee-Wee again?"

"The burn victim we pulled from the storage, the one we all thought was Lucky. He has a brother named Blood. They were the worst brother tandem the city ever had to deal with. They figured Blood and Lucky might be working together. Maybe they were right, or their cover was blown."

"Three more dead agents, and two of them were Secret Service. Next thing you know, they're going to ask me to step down as governor. What are our options?"

"I don't fuckin' know, but we don't have many. The press, the city are going to demand answers as to why we can't get over the hump and end the killing spree going against police officers and FBI agents."

"We need to come up with a quick solution. You don't have any other ideas, anything?"

"I do have one," the mayor said in a low tone, knowing the governor wouldn't approve. "Hear me out first. Maybe we need to release Captain Tuna and Speedy back out in the streets."

"What was that?" The governor got closer to the mayor and whispered in his ear, "Did you just say release Tuna and Speedy? That's the dumbest idea! Are you serious?"

The mayor took about three steps back. "Think about it. Lucky will come out the hole he's crawled into. It will basically be bait. We will just post bail for them and have them sit at home under house arrest."

"Then what?"

"We'll just watch Tuna and Speedy, and Lucky will show up. That's a guarantee."

The governor started walking in circles, holding his chin, thinking about the new proposal the mayor just threw at him. At first it sounded dumb, but the whole bait theory made sense. He walked back to the mayor.

"Okay, I'm going to agree with you on this one, but expect the city and the media to come down on you for the decision. They're going to eat you alive, and you won't be able to hide behind Richard for too long. You're going to have to face the press one day."

"I'm aware of the backlash, but once we finally capture Lucky, they will back off a bit," the mayor said in a confident tone.

They continued their conversation for a few more minutes before the governor left.

The mayor waited for Richard. Then they left together. On the way back to the office, he said to Richard, "We are going to authorize bail for both Tuna and Speedy, and get them back out in the streets. Lucky will show his face once he sees his two enemies released. He's not going to sit around while Tuna and Speedy are walking the streets of New York. Lucky wants them dead. We will need twenty-four-hour surveillance for both of them. Lucky will attack, and when he does, we'll be waiting."

"I like the idea, but are you ready to explain it to the city? The people are not going to take it lightly."

"It can't be any worse than the way they've been treating me these past few months. I don't have anything to lose. I have to resign on the last day of my term. What other choice do I really have but to put the pedal to the metal? If we capture Lucky, then the CIA will handle the rest. If this plan goes accordingly, the CIA will be able to help clear our image by exposing Lucky as a liar, whose plan was to set up the government." The mayor turned on the radio, a clear indication he didn't want to speak about it anymore.

Chapter 8

The Mayor's Last Desperate Move

The mayor needed the support of the governor in order for him to make calls and get the ball rolling. After a few phone calls, he set up a special arraignment the following morning. The judge was going to set bail at a million dollars apiece, and they both would be monitored by ankle bracelets and curfews upon their release.

After they arrived back at the mayor's office, Richard decided to leave. He couldn't take it anymore. He knew his boss was making a mistake by releasing Tuna and Speedy. The plan sounded good, but it was too risky.

Richard couldn't believe, with all the alleged corruption, that any government official would still do favors for the mayor. He was already bothered by the fact that he was kept in the dark about the assassination plot. He knew the mayor couldn't be trusted and would do whatever to clear his name. Richard knew it was time for him to look out for himself for once. He couldn't wait for the bomb to drop, because when the smoke cleared, the mayor would blame everything on him.

He decided to get in contact with Destine Diaz and start working on a plan of attack to clear his name. He pulled out his BlackBerry, found her number, and called her.

"This is Destine."

"Hello, Destine. This is Richard Claiborne."

Destine sat up in her chair and kicked everyone out of her office. She'd been waiting on his call for about four years now. "Surprise, surprise! I thought you didn't know my number, mister spokesperson," she said in a flirtatious voice.

"I didn't call to chitchat or catch up on things. Do you want the story of your life?"

"What do you have for me? You know I'm ready. You wouldn't call me if you thought I couldn't handle it," a cocky Destine shot back.

"I can't speak over the phone. We need to meet this evening, and not in public."

"Can you come by my place? I have a condo on twenty-second Street and Park Avenue. Can you stop by around nine, or is that too late?"

"That's perfect. I will call you when I'm outside, and please, no cameras or tape recorders."

"I promise," Destine said before she hung up the phone.

Destine couldn't believe the phone call she'd just received. Richard, always known as the mayor's pet, and a loyal one, too, was not known for sharing information. Destine knew the information had to be top secret. She couldn't wait till that night. She was upset she didn't say seven instead of nine. Destine didn't trust anyone in her office, or the entire building, for that matter, so she decided to keep the conversation with Richard to herself. She knew the media was a cutthroat business where you had to keep your story to yourself until you confirmed the facts and you had your name stamped on it, or the next reporter would steal your story.

Destine went about her day as usual and tried her best to ignore the clock.

Richard, on the other hand, was racing against time. He knew he had to relocate once he sat down with Destine and revealed the truth, but he was having second thoughts about it as well. He kept thinking about his family. It wasn't fair for them to move last minute and change their identities, and he wasn't sure they would understand.

Richard was upset that the mayor that kept him in the dark about Commissioner Fratt, but somehow he felt like he was committing a sin. On the other hand, if he didn't relocate and change his name, he would risk his freedom. Richard Claiborne wasn't built for the penitentiary and wasn't about to go to jail for the mayor. He was concerned his wife wouldn't bite on relocating. He was going to have to make a decision. But if he had to leave on his own, he would, since jail time wasn't an option. If he cooperated, he would be in the same position, anyway. His former boss would have him killed if he found out he was the one who leaked the information, and his family would have to go under protective custody. He just hoped his wife would roll with the plan.

As the day unfolded, it was getting worse for the mayor. While in his office, he received a call from Hilda Canton.

"Hello. It's Hilda. We are extremely disappointed on the current events. The president is overseas and will return shortly. He wanted me to express his frustration. It will be in your best interest to resolve this manhunt and gain control of your city before the president returns," she said.

"With all due respect, the president said he was leaving me the best two agents available, and they both were murdered with ease. Hopefully, he will understand what kind of monster we are dealing with. This character has already proved to be one of the most dangerous wanted men we have sought after. I need more help. Two agents won't get the job done. People are starting to call him the American bin Laden."

"Well, we'll just have to wait and see about that, but the question you should be asking yourself is, can you afford the wait?" Hilda hung up.

The mayor looked at the phone and didn't know how to take the threat. He didn't know if she meant they were going to fire or kill him. At that point, he didn't give a fuck. They had to get in line if they wanted to kill him. The mayor's only concern was capturing Lucky, and releasing Captain Tuna and Speedy was his last hurrah. If it backfired, he was going to kill himself, anyway. He wasn't about to face the embarrassment of corruption and possibly spending life in jail. If he killed himself, it would be easier for his family to move forward and mourn.

The mayor went home to spend time with his loved ones. He knew in the morning, after Tuna and Speedy were released on bail, he was going to face a media riot. He wanted to be well rested and maybe spend his last night at home with his wife and three daughters.

The governor didn't get a chance to go home and spend time with his wife and kids. He was too worried for the mayor. He knew his career was over. He wanted to save it before it was too late. Even though he agreed with the plan, he wanted to keep his involvement to a minimum. That way, if everything blew up in the mayor's face, it wouldn't affect him, but if it worked out, then, of course, he'd jump on the bandwagon and take credit for his involvement.

It was going to be a long night in New York City. Once word got out about the release of Captain Tuna and Speedy the next morning, the city would turn chaotic, especially after the Laura Coleman press conference where she made it clear on live TV about their plea deal and additional charges. The city was also right in the middle of negotiations with the Colemans on a lump sum settlement for the wrongful death of their son. How did you explain that the cops who pleaded guilty to manslaughter and were due in court for sentencing in four weeks were released on bail while fighting other corruption charges? It would actually set back the relationship between the city and its people, and erode the trust that was slowly building.

Lucky was glad to see Haze when he finally arrived after they went back and forth on the phone. Haze had been lost and couldn't understand the directions Lucky was giving him. After he arrived, Lucky showed him the apartment and wasted no time in getting ready to execute his next move.

"Listen, Haze, I don't have too much time to explain everything, but right now we need to go watch this apartment in downtown Manhattan."

"So let's go."

"You don't care who it is?"

"Nope. You called, and I came."

"That's gangsta. I could respect that. I'm thinking about kidnapping this reporter. I need her to record my side of the story."

"I understand. If you approached her straight up, she might call the boys on you. I'm with you."

"Exactly. So we are leaving in a few minutes." Lucky went in the room to freshen up and change his clothes.

It was going on nine o'clock. Destine was sitting on her sofa, sipping on Moscato, staring at her cell phone, waiting on Richard's call. Five minutes later, her phone started ringing.

"Hello," she answered in a sweet, low tone.

"It's me, Richard. I'm on the corner."

"My building number is seven hundred. I left your name with the doorman. Just show your ID, and he will give you access to the elevator. I'm on the last floor."

Right after Richard entered the building, Lucky, parked across the street, turned to Haze. "And the plot thickens," he said, rubbing both his hands together.

"Who is that, Lucky? He looks like a fed boy."

"That right there is the mayor's right-hand man, Richard Claiborne. There's no way he's hitting that, so I'm assuming he's there to drop a bomb. I guess he and the mayor are having a falling-out. This is perfect. I think we are going to have to switch our kidnapped target. I'm more interested in speaking to Richard than the reporter. This is why I love stakeouts. Listen and learn, li'l homie. Watch your enemies first before attacking them, and you will find better and easier strategies to eliminate them."

"Oh, I'm listening and learning. I still can't believe you're a cop. You like a hustler's mentor or some shit," Haze said in amazement.

"You like or watch sports?"

"Just football. I'm a die-hard Baltimore Raven fan."

"Perfect. I'm a Giant fan, but I'm a sports fan, period. You learn a lot from studying games and your opponents. I only study weaknesses, though, because that's how you beat the game, li'l homie. Offense is always good, but defense should always take precedence over everything. You feel me?"

"Got it."

Meanwhile Richard was upstairs spilling his guts. But before they began to speak, Destine had to be clear on his reasoning.

"So, tell me again," she said. "Why are you here? Are you pulling a trick on me?"

"No. I'm here because I could barely live with myself. I have protected this man for years, and I can no longer do it. I will not lie anymore."

"Okay, so what do you have for me that's so important? When you say 'this man,' are you talking about the mayor?" Destine thought that maybe Richard was just a bit crazy, and that she'd made a mistake inviting him to her apartment.

"Yes, this crazy man has arranged a secret hearing to set bail and release those bastards back into the streets."

"Are you referring to who I think you are? Are they letting those two dirty cops out on bail? Why? For what? Did you guys see the Colemans' press conference where she clearly stated they pleaded to manslaughter? You are going to release these two animals after all the mess they've caused?"

"Let me finish, Ms. Diaz. Why do you think I'm here? I don't agree with the decision. It was the mayor's idea, and the governor gave it the green light. They are hoping, by releasing Tuna and Speedy, they can make one last run at Lucky. I think the idea is dumb, especially after those three federal agents were killed."

"Are you serious? You mean both the governor and mayor are working together on this? I will be there tomorrow morning as they exit the courthouse. Secret, my ass. I'm glad you came forward. So, did Lucky really kill those three agents?"

"We don't know where he is. After he shot that officer in VA, we have had no contact. We don't know if he's still in Virginia or if he went to the fuckin' North Pole."

"What about those two agents killed on 117th Street?"

"Those two agents were assigned by the president himself. They were both ex-Navy SEAL, ex-secret agent, or some mess like that. Anyway, they were supposed to be the best. They were in the streets no more than a week, and they both were killed."

"Is the federal government helping on the situation? I saw Lucky was featured on *America's Most Wanted*. I know that must help."

"Both the FBI and the CIA are involved. There are all kinds of conspiracies going around."

"What kind of conspiracies? Are you referring to the assassination?"

"I won't get into details, but let's just say, Lucky wasn't the shooter."

"Are you serious? If he didn't kill the commissioner, then who did?"

"We're still trying to figure it out. The CIA knows who the shooter is, but they are not telling. We are clueless. I'm just trying to jump ship before it capsizes," Richard lied to her. He didn't want to say the mayor was responsible.

"And how deep is your neck tied up in this mess?"

"I made his dirty work look clean. I overlooked and turned my face on many occasions. I could have blown the whistle a long time ago, but when you know the information I know and how corrupt this city really is, you keep your mouth shut. I've seen informants disappear in thin air."

"So why are you speaking now?"

"Because the empire is crumbling and I'm going to disappear. I'm not going to stick around."

"What part of our conversation is off the record?"

"Well, I want you to show up at the arraignment tomorrow, but about the assassination, please keep that off the record. Well, at least give me about three to five days to clear all my accounts and move my family. After that, I don't care what you say, but please don't quote me."

"I will respect your wishes, and may God bless you. Would you like a glass of wine?"

"Oh no, thank you. I have to leave now. You be careful who you share this information with. It could cost you your life. Good night." Richard got up and let himself out.

Destine walked toward the door, shut it, and looked through the peephole, hoping Richard wouldn't come back and say he was playing. After a few seconds, she realized it was all true. She sat back on her sofa and poured another glass of wine. Her hand was shaking as she took a small sip of her Moscato. For the first time in her professional career, she had doubts and was scared. She had always wanted her shot, and this story could be it, but it came with a risk.

Then it finally hit her that Richard was leaving town because maybe the mayor was involved in the assassination.

***

As Destine sat there contemplating her next life-changing decision, Lucky was tailgating Richard.

Lucky turned to Haze. "At the next light, just pull up on the driver side. I'm going to try to jump in his car. Once I make my move, I want you to drive in front of him and block his path. Once I have control, just follow me. I'm not going to kill him unless he decides not to talk. He just left a reporter's house. I'm sure he was up there cooperating. Hopefully, he's still in a talkative mood. Okay, Haze, just roll up slow like an ordinary driver. I'll handle the rest."

As Haze pulled up next to Richard's black S600, Lucky quickly jumped out and stuck his gun through his half-open window.

"Turn the fuckin' car off and unlock the doors."

As soon as Richard noticed it was Lucky, he did as he said. He knew he was dealing with a killer and wasn't going to take any chances.

"Okay, I know who you are," Richard said as he turned his car off and unlocked the doors. "Please don't kill me. What do you want from me?"

As Lucky opened the door, he said, "Jump over to the passenger seat before I shoot your white ass."

Terrified, Richard jumped over.

Lucky jumped in and drove off while pointing his gun at Richard. Normally, he would knock out his victim, but Richard was no threat, so he gave him a break. He pulled over at the next available parking spot and then turned to him. "Okay, so why were you at that reporter's house?" he asked him as he pointed his gun at his face.

"Okay, wait. Don't shoot. I don't have any problems with answering all of your questions. You could actually just put the gun away. I want to help."

Lucky lowered his gun to make Richard feel more comfortable. "What was the meeting about?"

"Your ex-partners are getting out on bail, and the government is paying the bill."

"What? Are you fuckin' serious?"

"Yes, I am. The mayor is hoping this is their last shot at capturing you. He's pushing for one final plan. They want to charge you for the hit on the commish."

"But I didn't kill the commissioner. All I did was expose the truth."

"I'm about to tell you something that is top secret. Not even the feds are aware. I know you didn't kill the commissioner. It was Ralph. The mayor pulled off the hit. The CIA stopped by the office. They were the ones who figured out he was behind the hit. The CIA has agreed to help frame you, but the mayor has to do what no one has been able to do. Capture you."

"So the mayor hired the hit man, the CIA has proof, but somehow they still want to frame me?"

"That's correct. I'm done. I'm on my way home to pack, and I'm leaving town. If you have any more questions, now is the time."

"What is Destine going to do?"

"She'll be at the secret arraignment tomorrow morning with cameras. I want everyone to see how corrupt they are. Your best move is to disappear just like me."

"Who snitched on me? Who told ya about the storage facility?"

"I don't remember the girl's name."

"Where is she? Is she in protective custody?"

"No, she disappeared as well. Since she called the hotline, we haven't heard from her at all."

Lucky raised his gun and pointed it at Richard's face, erasing the confident swag he had three seconds ago.

"Listen to me carefully. Please don't make me shoot you. Where is she?"

"I swear to God, we don't know where she is," a frightened Richard quickly shot back.

Lucky had believed him the first time he said it, but he just wanted to make sure. He lowered his gun, and right before opening the door, he said, "If you tell anybody about this meeting, I will find and kill you."

"Don't worry, Lucky. I will be on the run myself. Thank you for sparing my life."

Lucky jumped out of the car and got back in the car with Haze, and they headed back uptown. Lucky decided to drive by the storage facility first. He wanted to see what kind of security was around. He needed to get his money out of there quickly, before a construction worker found it.

When they arrived there, he was surprised to see only one police cruiser on the block. Other than that, the property was burned to the ground, and was unprotected as well. That was all he needed to see. He decided to go in.

"Park right over there, Haze. Tonight is a perfect opportunity for me to go in. All you have to do is call me if you see the police cruiser move."

"A'ight, I got you."

Lucky got out of the car down the block and entered his storage facility through the back. The place still smelled like fire, and there was a lot of burned-up wood and trash all over the place. As he walked around, he thought about that fatal morning when he lost two friends. With every step he took, he was replaying the night. He could actually see Divine and Pee-Wee both holding guns, ready to die for him. It was a terrible feeling.

He finally reached his stash box. When he went to punch in the combination next to the door handle, he noticed it was already open. He quickly swung open the door and noticed the box was empty. All the money, drugs, and guns were gone.

Lucky stepped back and rubbed his head. "What the fuck! Where is my shit?" he asked himself, dumbfounded.

He snapped out of it and ran out of there like it was a setup. He jumped back in the car, and they drove off.

"My money, everything is missing, Haze. I don't know what the fuck is going on."

"What you mean, gone?"

"It's all gone, empty. Good thing Blood left me that money and guns behind. If not, we would have been fucked."

"Now what?"

"We are going back to the apartment while I try to figure out who stole my shit."

When they arrived back at the apartment, Lucky was mad as hell about his money. Different suspects ran across his mind. He logged on to the Net and checked his e-mail to see if Cyber Chris had found any information besides what Richard had already told him. When he logged on, he was happy to see that Cyber had finally sent him an e-mail, but he was disappointed after he read it. Cyber told him he was unable to break into the mayor's computer system, but he was able to get two very important addresses.

Since Cyber Chris didn't come through like he was supposed to, he didn't charge Lucky anything, not even for the little information he provided. But Lucky was still satisfied.

"Haze?"

"What's good, boss?"

"You don't need to call me that, Haze. I think I'm going to hold off on searching for Diamond out of town. I have a funny feeling she's still in New York and might've been behind my money vanishing. I can't think of no one else who could have done it. She's the last one alive who knows about the money, unless Sergio opened his big mouth to the CIA and they got me."

"How you know this bitch is involved?"

"Please, watch your mouth. I want her dead, but you don't have the rights to disrespect her. We clear?"

"My bad, boss. It won't happen again," Haze said, confused.

"Anyway, we are talking about a couple million dollars. That kind of money doesn't get stolen quietly. We just have to sit back and wait. Tomorrow morning will be a big day for us. Once the news camera catches these dirty cops leaving the courthouse, all hell will break loose. We'll just keep a low profile tonight and wait until the morning news."

Lucky was feeling like Blood, ready to explode and start killing everyone. He was really puzzled about who robbed him. He could only pray for their families, because they were all dead.

As he sat on the sofa, watching a movie, Haze came over and said, "Lucky, I need to talk to you, and I need your big brother advice."

"What's good, li'l homie? Talk to me."

"Back home, I been fuckin' with this chick for like six months. Right before I came up here, she told me she was knocked up. She's, like, three months now."

"Congratulations!"

"You see, that's the issue. I'm not ready to be a father. She's talking about not having an abortion. I'm not in love with this chick. We just been kicking it for, like, six months. I know I fucked up by not using a condom.

Shit! After a few months, I knew the pussy was mine, so I was just going raw. The pussy is good as shit, too."

"Ha! Ha! I feel you. Good pussy will make a man act unmoral. What kind of advice you want from me? If she's having it, then you going to have to step up and play the father role. You feel me?"

"We're not on the same page. I'm not ready to be a father, and she's not ready to be a mother. If she doesn't have the abortion, I'm going have to do the unthinkable." Haze grabbed the handle of the .38 on his hip.

"Slow the fuck down, Haze! You can't kill a pregnant woman. I understand you frustrated, but you have to find another solution."

"I need someone to talk her into an abortion."

"You sure the baby is yours?"

"I'm positive. I got shorty strung the fuck out. She's at my apartment right now, watching over my cousin. I left him there so he could serve my regulars. She's there to make sure my cousin don't fuck up and turn my place into a shit hole. She's a down-ass bitch, but we not ready to bring new life into this world."

"After this last job, with the kind of money I'm going to give you, you shouldn't have to sell drugs anymore. You could still be hustling, but running your own legit business. You could open a barbershop."

"I don't even know how to cut hair."

"You don't have to know. You could just run it and hire muthafuckas who know how to cut. Maybe open a clothing store. My point is simple. Having a baby will change your life, so you need to start making some life-changing decisions."

"But that's what I keep trying to tell her and you. I don't want to change my life. I'm up here with you, and you're the most wanted criminal in all of the United States. I'm here by choice. You didn't force me. If I had intentions of changing, I wouldn't be up here with you, ready to die."

"You're right, and I could respect that, but it's a little too late. The girl is pregnant. You can't kill her and the baby because you not ready to settle down. A man faces his responsibilities, not run from them. Trust me, I made the same mistake once with my daughter, and I wish I could take that decision back."

"What decision?" Haze asked.

"When my li'l girl was born, I didn't change. I was in the prime of my dirty career. I was making too much money and was snorting coke like a vacuum. Baby mama didn't take too lightly, and she bounced on me. For years, I blamed them and never once realized that it was me who pushed them away. For my ignorance, I lost time that I can't make up. You might be in the same situation."

"Trust me, I'm not. That bitch is dead if she doesn't get an abortion. I hear what you saying, but I thought you would be more on my side. If you ask me to kill someone, I wouldn't ask why. I will just do it. I don't understand why you can't side with me on this one."

"You asked for my advice, li'l homie. I don't just say what people want to hear. I say what's on my mind. Killing her would make things worse, especially if you get caught. You rather spend the rest of your life being in jail than being a father? That's crazy."

"It sounds crazy, but if you were in my shoes and at my age, you would be thinking the same. This bitch is trying to trap me, and I can't let her. I'm going in the room. I need to lay down and think about this shit here."

"A'ight, li'l homie, you will make the right decision," Lucky said to boost his spirits. "You will see."

Haze went in the room and closed the door behind him. He dropped backward on the bed, then stared at the ceiling, pondering his next move. He knew Lucky made sense, but he just didn't want to accept the reality.

Haze's childhood wasn't the greatest. He knew his parents weren't ready for him and his sister. Their upbringing was rough and came with a great deal of embarrassment. He remembered a lot of hungry nights, and kids at school making fun of their clothes and hairstyles.

Haze, at an early age, had to learn how to defend himself on his own. His father never spent time with him, and by the time he was seven, his father already had disappeared. Three years later his mother died of AIDS.

From then on, Haze bounced around from family house to shelter until he was about sixteen years old. That's when he went to Job Corps, where he acquired survival tactics and the tools to be successful. Haze utilized the job program as a benefit to find shelter and gain an education.

After a year and a half, Haze returned to Glen Burnie, Maryland. He'd made a weed connect while in Job Corps, and when he went back, he called him up and from that day on never looked in the rearview mirror.

Haze lost contact with his sister about four years ago. He tried hard to locate her but was unsuccessful.

As Haze lay on that bed and dwelled on the past, thinking about his sister made him emotional. Those feelings led him to see Lucky's point. It was not worth killing his baby mama and risk going to jail for life.

Haze walked back out to the living room, where Lucky was still watching TV. "You are right, Lucky," he said. "It's time I become a man and handle my responsibilities. When I get back home, the change is coming with me. Thanks for making me realize the reality of my actions. It's not like if I own my business and pay taxes, I'm a square. I don't have to be a thug to gain respect."

"I'm glad you came to your senses. If I didn't believe in you, I wouldn't have given you real advice."

"That's why I approached you, because you will keep it real. I'm going back to the room to get some sleep."

"A'ight. I'm going to stay up for a bit. I'll see you in the morning."

As Lucky lay across the sofa, channel surfing, he couldn't stop thinking about who stole his money. He went through his list of suspects. Diamond couldn't pull off the job alone, even though she was a great student. Lucky knew, somehow, there was a twist or a surprise. He just couldn't figure what it was. In his mind, the only person who could have helped her was Sergio.

Lucky sat up and thought to himself, *Damn! We didn't even check Sergio's apartment.* He jumped up and was about to get dressed. Then he paused. *I'm bugging. With that kind of money and product, it would have been visible.*

He sat back down on the sofa, but his mind kept playing tricks on him. He was breathing hard, and his heart was pounding out of his shirt. He went to the kitchen and poured himself a glass of cold water. After drinking the water, he leaned his head against the kitchen cabinet and let his mind work.

Next on his list was the CIA. They were capable of pulling off the job. But, to Lucky, it seemed too easy to pick them. He couldn't put it past them, since they were known for their dirty tactics as well. Lucky knew there was a third suspect involved, but he just couldn't figure out who. And it was killing him inside, since no one else knew about the money.

Lucky started banging his head against the cabinet.

Haze came out of the room and walked toward him. "Are you all right, Lucky? Why are you banging your head against the cabinet?"

"I'm good. I'm just trying to figure out who the fuck stole my money."

"I thought you said it was either Diamond or the CIA."

"I know, but there's a third person missing, and I can't figure out who it is."

"No disrespect, but what about Blood? He look grimy. Did he know about the money?"

"I can't lie. I thought about it, but I just can't see it. He would have called the cops on me. I don't see it. You feel me?"

"I feel you. So are you good? I'm going back to bed."

"I'm good. Good night, li'l homie." Lucky walked in the bedroom as well to get some rest.

It was going on three in the morning, and Lucky couldn't fall asleep. For some strange reason, he decided to call Tasha. It would be the first time he'd be calling her since leaving Atlanta. He was scared to make the phone call, but he knew he had to make it.

He dialed her number. Her phone rang six times, and then it went to voice mail. He hung up and dialed the number again.

"Hello."

"Baby, it's me," Lucky said.

Tasha said, "Hold on." She got up because Tamika was in the bed with her. She walked over to the kitchen area. "Lucky, what the fuck? You finally decided to call? What the hell have you started? Did you kill the commissioner?"

"No, baby."

"I thought you were going to New York. Why the fuck were you in Maryland? You were looking for that other bitch? You fuckin' another bitch and I'm down here waiting on you. Fuck you, Lucky! You're not going to change."

"Please, baby, let me talk for a second. I did not kill the commish. The mayor did. I was down in Maryland, following some leads. Somebody stole my money. I'm almost done. I'll be down there soon. Give me a few more days. How is Tamika?"

"Don't switch up the conversation. Why can't you leave right now? They had you on *America's Most Wanted.*"

"C'mon, how's Tamika?"

"She can't stop talking about you. Every day she asks me if you call and when you coming home."

"Damn! That's why I didn't want to call. Anyway, you make sure you tell her that her daddy loves the shit out of her and that I'm sorry I made the wrong decision in the past."

"You could tell her when you get here. I don't understand why you can't just walk away, but I understand my man. So, hurry the fuck up and stay alive. We miss you, Donald."

"I miss you guys more. Love you. Good night. I'm going to bed. I will call you."

"Good night. *Mwa!*"

Chapter 9

Bail Is Set

As the sun came up, Lucky was already on the floor, doing push-ups, and getting ready for the day. First thing he did after his workout was turn on the TV. It was going on six thirty in the morning. When he went to knock on the guest room door, Haze came out sweaty. He was also in there working out. Lucky loved the kid's dedication.

"I thought I was going have to come in there and wake you up."

"Not me. I'm learning from the best. It's only right I follow your routine to the T."

They both went to the living room to watch TV. They weren't going to move until they saw Destine Diaz with cameras on those pigs' faces when they left the courthouse.

The mayor was at home having a nervous breakdown. He started having second thoughts about his decision to set Tuna and Speedy free. After spending the night at home with his family, he realized how much he didn't want to end up in jail. His wife wouldn't be able to handle the pressure of holding the family down on her own.

The mayor didn't mind losing his job. His loss of freedom was his biggest concern. The CIA knew he was responsible for pulling off one of the most brazen attacks against the city of New York. He had everything to lose and was backed against the wall. That was the reason why he'd decided to take yet another risk and release both Tuna and Speedy. The mayor was basically showing his selfishness. He was concerned only about his freedom and safety. If the plan was effective, he would at least guarantee his get-out-of-jail card.

He didn't care about the safety of either Tuna or Speedy. He knew their lives were in danger. At least in jail, while under protective custody, Lucky wouldn't be able to touch them, but in the street was a different story. Lucky had already proved to be a determined hunter, and unstoppable, too.

The mayor was almost certain Lucky would go after Tuna and Speedy. Before he left his house and headed to his office, his wife gave him a kiss and hug, something she hadn't done in a long time. It felt awkward, like his wife knew today would make or break their family and future.

As he walked toward his car, again he started second-guessing himself, but it was too late. All the chips were already in place. The hearing was set for seven in the morning, right before the morning court rush. The mayor wasn't going to be present. He went into his office. He was going to let Richard be his eyes and ears, and face the press afterward.

The governor, who'd also had a long night, joined the mayor at his office.

"I couldn't sleep. How about you, Ralph?" the governor asked.

"I haven't slept, either. We can't pull the plug now. I just hope this last attempt doesn't backfire on us," the mayor said in a low, sleepy voice.

"What about the media? Are they still in the dark?"

"So far they are. I haven't heard from Richard. That usually means the media still don't know. It won't take them long, though."

"I just don't want the media present at the hearing or near the courthouse," the governor shot back.

"Don't worry. We should be fine."

They continued their short talk as they killed time. It was going on seven in the morning, and they both were on the sofa, watching the morning news.

The mayor was a bit worried that he hadn't heard from Richard. He tried calling his cell phone, but it went straight to voice mail. The mayor couldn't remember the last time Richard's phone went straight to voice mail.

Around seven fifteen in the morning, right after the weather report, anchorman John Silverman came on.

"Good morning, New York. In a few minutes, we will be coming live from the front steps of the supreme court down in Manhattan. Destine Diaz will report live on a breaking story that will sure shock all New Yorkers. Please stay tuned."

Both the mayor and governor looked at each other. They picked up their cell phones and started making calls.

The mayor called Richard numerous times but got no answer, so he called his secretary. She also hadn't heard from Richard. The mayor was beginning to sweat.

He turned toward the governor to see if he was able to reach out to any of his people. "I wasn't able to reach Richard. Have you heard from the DA or anybody else?" the mayor asked.

"No, I haven't. This is not good. How in the hell did the media find out about this so quick? We have a leak in our team. We need to head down to the courts right now. Once New Yorkers see these two police officers walking out the courtroom, their lives might be in jeopardy."

"Well, let's see what the report is about first," the mayor said, trying to bring calm to the situation.

"C'mon, Ralph, we both know what the report is about. Why would they be at the court steps?" The governor was furious.

The mayor didn't reply, because he was right. They both sat back down and waited like the other millions of viewers.

Speculation was rife around the local coffee shops and breakfast locations. Everyone thought they'd finally caught Lucky, who had turned into public enemy number one. After the assassination and the riots, the love for Lucky had vanished, and the people had actually started blaming him for everything. However, the catch-22 was that those two rogue cops roaming the streets, free on bail, proved Lucky's point—New York was a corrupt city.

The Colemans, along with Kim, were watching the news as well. They were also crossing their fingers, hoping they didn't catch Lucky. As they sat in suspense, so did Lucky and Haze.

Right before Lucky was about to get up for a glass ofS juice, the news came back on. He jumped back on the couch and turned the volume up.

"Welcome back. I'm John Silverman. Before the break, I reported we have an exclusive report with reporter Destine Diaz, who's down at city hall."

"Thank you, John. I'm here on the steps of the Supreme Court of the State of New York, where we

expect to see Captain William 'Tuna' Youngstown and Detective Jeffrey 'Speedy' Winston, labeled the worst rogue cops in NYPD history. They have already pleaded guilty to manslaughter charges in the Perry Coleman case and have numerous charges pending, including murder, drug trafficking, money laundering, and all sorts of other corruption charges. They were sitting in jail with no bail, but somehow this morning, about five minutes ago, they were in a secret arraignment approved by the mayor himself, and they both received bail, which was paid within seconds after the ruling.

"We will try to interview these officers as they exit the courthouse. After what the city has gone through, I'm not sure New Yorkers will be able to handle yet another government scandal. Releasing these two officers will cause an ugly stir.

"I think the officers are walking out right now. Let's see if we can get any answers."

Destine walked up the steps with her camera crew to get a closer look at Tuna and Speedy. When Tuna walked out of the courthouse, another man threw a jacket around his head and rushed him down the steps.

"Detective Jeffrey Winston, can you please answer a few questions?"

Speedy actually stopped when Destine called his name. *"Please, call me Speedy,"* he said in a stressful voice.

"Okay, Speedy, what happened in there? How did you guys manage to get bail, and who paid for it?"

"I don't know what happened. I was told by the correction officer last night that I had court today. I didn't know, and I didn't pay the bail."

"Then who paid the bail, Speedy?"

Speedy looked straight into the camera and slowly said, *"Taxpayers. Who else do you think paid the bail?"* He pushed the camera aside and walked away, ignoring Destine's calls.

"Well, there you have it, New York. These cops were set on bail with your tax dollars, according to Detective Jeffrey 'Speedy' Winston, one of the prime suspects in one of the worst corruption trials in New York history.

"Again, the two police officers, who were labeled rogue cops and were sitting in jail with no bail, were just released on bail. I'm referring to Captain Tuna and Detective Speedy. We will have more on this story as it develops. This is Destine Diaz, reporting live from city hall. Back to you, John."

Everybody who just heard the report went ballistic, many feeling double-crossed by the city once again, especially right after the riots. It was another setback.

The Colemans were beyond shocked. Laura herself stayed frozen. It took her husband almost a minute to get her to snap out of it.

"What the hell just took place, honey? Did I just see Tuna and Speedy walk out of the courthouse?"

"Those crooked bastards!" Perry Sr. said. "How can they give them bail and then try to have a secret arraignment? I'm glad the reporter was there and recorded them leaving out the hearin'."

"Once we get our money, I want to move as far away from New York as we can."

"What about Perry's body?"

"We'll have Perry's body transferred to whatever city we move to. I'm tired. I don't have the energy to fight anymore. Let them roam free in the street. I hope Lucky kills both of them."

"Laura, how can you say that?"

"All I wanted was for these officers to pay for what they done. Now they get a chance to sit at home while they go through another trial. Oh Lord, I'm sorry. Please pardon my behavior. I'm tired of playing Mrs. Good Lady, Jesus. How much longer does this nightmare last? I just want to move away, honey." Laura threw her body on the sofa in surrender.

Meanwhile, the mayor and governor were both throwing tantrums. They couldn't believe they'd really allowed Tuna and Speedy to walk out the front door.

"Where the fuck is Richard? How could they walk right out the front doors? Richard would never allow that to happen."

"Well, that didn't go well, did it? Not a good start for the final hurrah. Where is Richard? You think maybe he's the one who blew the whistle?"

"Who? Richard? I don't think he would cross me like that. We've been friends for over twenty years."

"Well, I'm sorry to be the one to break the bad news to you, but I think your boy gave us up. He's the only one who's unaccounted for at this moment. Did you guys have any type of confrontation?"

"Well, sort of, but it was nothing. Maybe you're right about him blowing the whistle, but until I speak to him, I'll hold my judgment."

"Fair enough, but you need to get in contact with him soon."

***

Lucky and Haze were watching TV with smiles on their faces.

"You see, Haze, all you have to do is sit back and watch everything unfold. It's like playing chess by yourself. You feel me? These idiots are making it easier for me. I'm going to hunt down Tuna and Speedy and kill them both."

"Ha! Ha! Let's do it. Are we also going after Diamond?"

"I'm more concerned about killing my ex-partners. Right now, I don't give a fuck about my money or Diamond. Tuna and Speedy, those are the only two names I want to hear around this muthafucka. Wait, did I just say I don't care about Diamond? I must be high."

"I was going to say something, boss, but—"

"My bad. While we hunting down these two cocksuckas, I'm going to have my peoples hunt down Diamond. I have a connect over in Motor Vehicle."

Lucky stood up, logged in the computer, and sent another e-mail to Asia, asking her to do a national search on Diamond's real name. He wanted her to check hotel reservations, flights, car rentals, real estate, rental properties, and bank accounts, if possible. Asia was good at what she did and had connects that could perform the kind of search Lucky was requesting.

As he was typing, Haze walked over and read the e-mail. "Is this bitch that good?"

"Who? Asia? She's the best. She would slap the shit out of Waldo and tell him to step his game up. That's how good she is. Once we know what city she's at, we will make our move. If she did take the money, she'll make a mistake. That's too much money for a female not to get tempted to spend in a wild shopping spree."

"You're right about that. She will go shopping. But what you mean, 'if she did take the money'?"

"Well, remember I told you right before we killed Sergio, we seen two suits walking out the building? Sergio confirmed they were CIA agents. Who knows what he told them. If he mentioned the money, then I know they went and retrieved it."

"That make sense. So who took your money? The CIA or Diamond?"

"That's the million-dollar question. If the CIA took the money, they would have brought it to my attention already. They would have used it as leverage. I didn't see any notes lying around. Maybe they'll use the media and send a message. If Diamond took the money, then her name will pop up somewhere."

"If you had to bet, who would you pick?"

"Diamond. Her and Sergio had this mapped out for a long time. I feel worse than I did before. She betrayed me. Once I catch this girl, hell will seem like paradise after I'm done with her ass. I'm going to torture her for like two days."

"Two days? Damn! I feel sorry for her already. Well, I'm about to roll up and get my mind right while you wait for Asia to get back at you." Haze got up and went back in the guest room to handle his business.

Lucky sat there in front of the computer and was browsing the Internet while he waited on Asia's reply. It was still early in the day, and he figured Asia should respond any minute now.

The TV caught his attention when the news showed clips of different political figures displaying their disappointment in the latest collapse within the government. It was obvious to the naked eye that Captain Tuna and Detective Speedy should have never had their bail status changed.

Every time Lucky thought about it, he laughed to himself. "The mayor has finally fucked his own self in the ass." All he could hope for was that the city would start to reconsider its quick judgment on him. He could never be considered a hero, but he was damn near close to one. He did what many wouldn't have done. He risked his life to tell the truth, not once, twice, or three times, but a bunch of times.

As Lucky was about to start making something to eat, he noticed he had a new e-mail. It was from Asia. She told him that Diamond was given a speeding ticket in Little Rock two days ago. That was perfect news. He didn't need to send Haze out there first. He could go and find her himself.

He called Haze back in the living room.

"What's going on, boss?"

"I told you about calling me that. Anyway, Asia just replied to my e-mail and said Diamond was given a speeding ticket near her hometown in Arkansas."

"So, when are we leaving? Tonight?"

"Nah. At least we know where she's at. I don't have to send you out there first. As bad as I want to find Diamond, my ex-partners are first on the list. I might not get another shot at them. They're both facing hard time."

As Lucky went over the new plan with Haze, the mayor was in his office, preparing to face the media and give a statement. He still hadn't seen or heard from Richard, whom he could always rely on to face the media and take the bullets he dodged.

The mayor knew something was off, because he even called Richard's home number and there was no answer. Maybe Lucky got to him and killed his whole family. Worried, he called his secretary and told her to send a police car to Richard's home.

The mayor would have never thought his good friend was actually the rat, as the governor pointed out.

As he continued to sweat, trying to prepare the statement of his life for the press, his secretary called his phone. The CIA was back at the office and wanted to see him. He almost caught a heart attack. He fixed his tie and opened the door.

Agent Scott Meyer and Agent Marie Summit stormed in and slammed the door behind them.

"Don't walk in my office in that manner. What's the problem? I thought Richard gave you guys all the files you needed."

"Well, that's why we are here. You are not keeping your end of the bargain. We don't have all the files. We haven't heard from Richard. Where is he?" Agent Meyer asked.

"If you find him, let him know I'm looking for him as well."

"Are you saying he's AWOL, Your Honor?" Agent Meyer asked.

"Correct."

"That's not good. What's this new mess about releasing those two dirty cops? You're making it harder for us to clear your name out this mess."

"Well, that's basically my last attempt at capturing Lucky. You guys want me to capture him, so that's what I'm doing. All we have to do is watch Captain Tuna's and Detective Speedy's homes, and Lucky will appear. He will make an attempt at killing both of them, and we'll be waiting."

"I will admit, I like your plan. The clock is ticking. You have about seventy-two hours before our offer expires. We also have new intel that may help your investigation. We tracked down who really called in the storage tip. It wasn't his female protégée. One of

Lucky's students set everything up to steal the money he had stashed in the storage. His name is Sergio.

"Sergio had his girlfriend call and pose as Diamond. Of course, he was hoping nothing would be traced back to him. He just wasn't as smart as he thought he was. He should have never used his cell phone."

"That's great news. You mean to tell me a former student is willing to help us?"

"*Was.*"

"What you mean, was?" the mayor asked, looking at both Meyer and Summit.

"We went back to his apartment, and we found him dead. He was tortured pretty bad. We're assuming Lucky saw us when we stopped by the first time."

"There goes the great news. What the fuck happened? Why you guys didn't protect him? How can ya leave him there? He was a prime witness. We could have protected him."

"Sergio told us Lucky went to his apartment after the storage shooting and then headed down to Maryland to look for his protégée, but she's actually back home in Little Rock, Arkansas. Her real name is Tracey Sanders or Stevens. He wasn't sure. Lucky believes she's the one who leaked the information. He wants revenge. Sergio also said that Lucky's ex-girlfriend and daughter are now living in Atlanta. Lucky is not back in town just for revenge. He has a couple million dollars stashed in the storage facility."

"Well then, his money burned with everything else," the mayor said.

"Not exactly, sir. According to Sergio, Lucky had a fireproof room. We went back to search for this secret room. We found it, but it was empty. No money or drugs."

"Damn! He already got his money?"

"We don't think so. We're following other leads, but Sergio was after his money, as was Diamond. Maybe she went back, who knows."

"That's great to know. I could use that as bait. I can't believe he moved his family so quick. I really hope you are right about him not having his money, because he if does, he's long gone."

"Sergio also said that the day the commissioner was assassinated, he found Lucky passed out on his roof. He said Lucky had snorted so much cocaine, he passed out naked with his rifle by his hand and doesn't remember what happened that morning. It should be easy for us to pin everything on him."

The mayor's eyes opened up like a little kid's on Christmas morning. "That's fuckin' perfect. If he was found like you said, then it should be easy."

"Not so fast," Agent Summit said, finally breaking her silence. "You have to catch Lucky first, which obviously for you is hard to do."

The mayor looked at Agent Summit up and down. "When you see men conversing, please play your role and be quiet." He then turned back toward Agent Meyer. "I feel confident we will catch Lucky within forty-eight hours. I will call you if otherwise. Now, please, let me show you to the door. I have a press conference in a few minutes."

As both agents were walking out of his office, the mayor checked with his secretary to see if the police had arrived at Richard's home.

"Nothing yet, sir," she answered.

The mayor walked back in his office and started adding the finishing touches to his prepared remarks for his press conference.

***

Meanwhile, the news stations were already reporting that the press conference was taking place.

The mayor wasn't focused at all, with all the new info he had, and couldn't wait to start making moves. He could get the FBI to locate Lucky's family in Atlanta, while he followed up with his female protégée, who was still unaccounted for. Now they had her real name and the city where she was from. That should be an easy find.

There were all kinds of news reporters outside of city hall. New Yorkers were concerned with the new direction because, so far, it was still looking like the old corrupt one. The people were again demanding more assurance. The mayor's word wasn't good anymore. They didn't understand why those police officers had been released.

The mayor had about another thirty minutes before walking out to the podium. All of New York was once again glued to their TVs, radios, and logged on the Internet.

The Colemans were watching, and so were Lucky and Haze.

Lucky just wanted to hear what blame would be thrown his way.

Chapter 10

The Mayor's Press Conference

The mayor was going to update the city on recent developing stories. Richard wasn't around, but he'd sure picked up a few tricks watching Richard handle the press. He was going to use the press conference as his last plea to win the city back. As the time got closer to face the press, the mayor began to sweat heavily once again. He looked like he had run on the treadmill for ten miles with a three-piece suit on. What also made him nervous was the fact that the governor wasn't present. He was hoping they didn't kill him.

The mayor walked toward the podium, praying and asking God to forgive him. As he got closer to the microphone, he kept looking around, trying to locate any snipers. Before he even opened his mouth, spectators were already yelling obscene language at him. Those yelling obscenities were removed by the NYPD, according to their no tolerance code, and there were extra police present to prevent any outburst.

"Good afternoon. I want to thank everyone who waited so patiently. I'm here today to speak on certain matters that are slowing down our process in growing as a community. Especially after the riots, we need to put our differences to the side and stick together. It's easy to point fingers, but harder to stand up and make a change. I'm not here to place blame on anyone. However, I do take responsibility for everything. All the conspiracy theories of corruption happened under my watch. I accept the criticism. I watch the news and read the paper. I hear the harsh comments thrown my way. All I can say is that every day I gave it my all. I spent hours on top of hours serving this great city. I missed so many family functions because I'm in the streets, shoulder to shoulder with the people running the city. That being said, ladies and gentlemen, let's get down to business.

"I first want to give the final update on the Perry Coleman case. I know recent events have the minds of many wondering. The officers involved, Captain Tuna and Detective Speedy, have pleaded guilty to manslaughter charges and their guilty plea has not been revoked. I believe in six weeks they are getting sentenced for that case. They are each getting nine years to life. As we know, their civil case was already settled.

"The Coleman case was a tragedy and a wake-up call for all. Because of the outcome of the case, the NYPD has implemented new training for the cadets. These training classes will teach our officers how to use multiple tactics of restraining a suspect without the use of their handguns. I'm deeply sorry for the shooting. We lost a good man and great father. Perry Coleman, may God bless your soul and the souls of your loved ones. From the city of New York and the entire police department, we apologize."

The mayor paused and sipped on a glass of water. He kept looking around, trying to find the shooter. He knew for sure that in only a matter of seconds from he would hear the sound of a gunshot that would put him out of his misery.

The opening part of the mayor's statement caught everyone off guard, and now they were listening with open ears. Even Laura Coleman, who was at home watching, thought it was a nice gesture. He was fooling everyone, and it was working.

"I will also update everyone about those famous envelopes that shocked us all. We have information that leads us to believe Lucky was responsible for mailing out these envelopes. His plans were to expose the government for corruption. I just want to give everyone an update on those accusations. In the case against Rell Davis, I'm glad to announce this matter has been settled as well. We cleaned his criminal record, including previous charges that were not relevant to his last case. He will get a chance to start a new life. Also, Captain Tuna, Detective Speedy, and Detective Lucky are now facing double murder charges for the death of Rodger and Connie Newton. Each count of murder carries a twenty-five to life maximum sentence. It seems like in Rell's case, the city failed to live up to its constitutional standards, and for that, I also apologize. I will say that his settlement was one of the highest we ever paid, right behind what we gave the Coleman family. They will get a chance to move forward and start the healing in peace.

"The next envelope involved the case of Juan 'Pito' Medina. I'm not going to get into too many details on his situation because of an ongoing appeal. We are still fighting his situation. This is a dangerous man who, we believe, belongs behind bars for life. I want the city to please not place this man on the same pedestal as Rell Davis. We understand there were some questionable tactics performed in his arrest, but we are talking about a drug kingpin. He was still running his operation while incarcerated. Even behind bars, he's still responsible for most of the cocaine moving in and out of Washington Heights and all the gang-related murders. If we let Pito walk out of jail, the drug and murder rate will increase dramatically. This man is a monster.

"The envelope involving the Wiggins family is also still under investigation. The Wiggins are not participating in the investigation. They have chosen to remain silent. It's hard for me to give any update, or confirm the raid that killed one and left another paralyzed actually took place. Without their cooperation and no evidence, I can't update this case. I will say we are still investigating the matter at full force.

"There were also allegations of corruption against the late Commissioner Brandon Fratt. The commissioner was prepared to resign and fight for his freedom through our judicial system. The assassination prevented that from happening, and we were all left puzzled. He's not alive to defend himself. We are still conducting our investigation on the allegations against him. But, at the moment, that's all we are doing, just gathering information. We will make public what we can. I'm not giving him any special treatment. If he was corrupt, then he will be exposed.

"I also want to address the allegation against the cardinal Joseph King III. This case is a personal one, because as we all know this man married my wife and me. He baptized my kids. He ate dinner at my house many times. We have taken vacations together. I have let my own kids stay over at his house. However, I do want to address the critics. It is absurd to imagine that I knew of his secret life, if the allegations are true. In no way would I support child pornography.

"The cardinal's trial is set to start within a few months. I haven't spoken to the man since the charges went public. If there are videos of him with underage boys, I don't need to hear his side. There is no explanation for such devilish acts. It upsets me when I hear comments about how I'm good friends with the cardinal. I'm here today to say, that's not the case. I will not interfere with the case, nor will I provide any type of support. We are not friends.

"Let's talk about a more serious issue. We're currently still in search of Donald Gibson, better known as Lucky. This man is wanted and is considered armed and dangerous. Please don't help hide this criminal. Call us today if you know his whereabouts. His name has been cleared from the Coleman case, but he's still a suspect in about ten other murders. He's the prime suspect in the assassination of the commissioner. Right now, our main concern is capturing Lucky. Lucky, if you are listening, I have a few messages for you. We have your money you left behind at the storage facility, and we are also in Atlanta, looking for some of your old friends."

The mayor paused and took another sip of water. He looked around again but felt more confident that he wasn't about to get shot. He knew if Lucky was watching, he was shitting in his pants when he heard him mention Atlanta.

"I felt it was important for me to come out today to personally speak on incidents that shook up our great city. I wanted to assure everyone that we will not stand for it anymore. We will change and turn this horrific page and begin our new chapter. Especially after the riots, we need to rebuild our bond, our confidence among each other. We can only do it if we stick together and work as a team.

"I know there have been whispers about me as well. I read the papers and listen to the radio shows. The comments hurt, and they hurt my family as well. My kids get taunted every day in school. My wife, the other night at Bible study, had to answer questions about my character. Please, leave my family alone. Call me all the names you want, but attacking my family is out of line. I can't let these distractions get in my way of running this city.

"Yes, I'm hurt, but I can't show my emotions. I can't stand up here, start to cry, and beg for your forgiveness. I'm not a quitter, and I'm here to fight till the end. I won't be forced to resign on false allegations. Once we capture Lucky, the truth will come out and put a lot of these accusations in perspective. But, again, I take full responsibility.

"I will now do something mayors usually don't do. I will open up the floor to a few questions. If I feel like the question doesn't need an answer, then I will say, 'Next question,' and we will move on. The longer you guys respect the rules, the longer I'll stand here. You guys start to ask anything out of context, I will walk away."

All the reporters present were shocked that the mayor opened up the floor for questioning. They were all looking around at each other. It took about ten seconds for the first question to come out.

"Mr. Mayor, Chris Whitley from the *City Paper*. Can you explain how Tuna and Speedy received a new bail hearing? Can you please elaborate on it?"

"I hear the outcries about police officers receiving special treatment, but that's not the case. These officers have dedicated their entire lives to protecting civilians. They risk their lives every day they put on those uniforms. A lot of these allegations will get cleared once we capture Lucky and prove he masterminded this whole corruption theory."

"So are you saying Lucky is really behind all the corruption? That he is the one responsible for setting up our government?"

"Exactly. But I will hold my judgment until we capture Lucky. I don't want to make any overstatements. We feel highly confident things will turn for the better once we truly have him in custody."

"Your Honor, I'm Susan Murray with Channel Seven News. Do you have leads on Lucky? So far he's been able to elude the police in every attempt and more officers are losing their lives, including federal agents."

"I'm aware of the losses this city has suffered, and my prayers are with the families. We are not in business to lose police officers or FBI agents. That's unacceptable. With regards to the prime suspect, well, let's just say Lucky has been real lucky. We have reasons to believe his run will come to an end very soon. We are working around the clock to bring him to justice, and we will this time around."

"Your Honor, what do you say to those who consider Lucky a hero?" another reporter asked.

"I don't consider him a hero, do you?" the mayor asked the young reporter.

The reporter didn't reply to the question. He just looked at the mayor with a blank expression.

The mayor bailed him out by not waiting on his answer. "Listen, I'm not going to stand here and say that I haven't heard the word *hero* thrown around. I refuse to accept that. This man has admitted to abusing his authority and disgracing his badge. He's a cocaine addict, has committed murder, sold and stole guns, distributed drugs, and the list continues. I know, in my book, no one with that kind of résumé is considered a hero. Next question," an annoyed mayor said.

"Are you considering resigning in the midst of all the corruption allegations?"

"No. Didn't you hear the press conference? I made that clear. C'mon, guys, any real questions?"

"Are you running again when your term expires?" the same reporter asked.

"I haven't made that decision. Look, if the city feels like they want a new face to sail the ship, I would understand. I'm not a quitter. I'm not resigning. But I understand if the city needs a new voice. I'm just trying to make sure I clean up the mess made under my watch."

"Mr. Mayor, what last message of hope do you have for the people who are at home watching?"

"Please be patient, please have faith, and we will all turn the corner in triumph. Thank you for coming out today, and God bless you," the mayor said as he walked away.

As the mayor left, a few reporters were still asking questions, which went unanswered. The mayor jumped in a waiting black Suburban truck and headed back to his office. While in the car, he called his secretary to find out if she had an update on Richard.

"Sorry. Nothing yet. The police searched his house. No one was home. His neighbors stated they saw them load up the family van like they were going on a vacation."

"Okay, thank you." The mayor hung up the phone.

The mayor finally realized that the governor was correct about Richard. He didn't want to believe it at first, but it was obvious Richard jumped ship on the team. He felt betrayed but understood maybe his good friend was upset about the assassination plot. He just couldn't believe he would go to the media instead of having a conversation with him. Richard was the least of his problems at the moment, so he brushed it to the side. He needed to refocus and pull it together.

He went to visit Captain Tuna and Speedy at their homes to discuss their next move. While on his way to Long Island, he called up the governor.

"Ralph, about time you called. The press conference was excellent. You looked and sounded sincere. I did notice you kept looking around as you spoke. Did you think you were going to get shot?"

"Ha! Of course I did. I was looking around for snipers. I was scared to death standing on that podium. What's the overall feedback? Positive or negative?"

"I would say half and half. I would guarantee you, your press conference helped ease the mind of a lot of voters, especially as you opened up the floor for questions. That took a lot of guts."

"I was just trying to be as authentic as possible. I'm buying us some time to catch this son of a bitch. I'm on my way to Tuna's house first, then Speedy's. They're both under house arrest. As a matter of fact, I'm going to wait until the morning to visit them."

"What's the plan?"

"That's the plan. Making sure they stay home, and we wait for Lucky to make his move."

"That's it?" the governor asked, confused.

"That's it. Lucky will come for them, trust me."

"I hope everything goes that easy. Call me after you visit both of them tomorrow and give me the latest update." The governor ended the call.

Lucky was walking back and forth in the living room. He couldn't believe the police knew where Tasha and Tamika were. He thought Sergio must have told them.

"Fuck, Haze! They know where my family is at."

"Oh, that's why the mayor said Atlanta? I guess we also know who took your money."

"I have to call Tasha and tell her to get the fuck out of Atlanta. They will find her quicker than me going down there. These muthafuckas took my money, and now they're going to take my family. I don't think so."

"So let's start taking theirs," Haze said.

"That's a good idea. I know the mayor has a few daughters. Fuck!" Lucky yelled at the top of his lungs. "This changes everything. Oh, they're going to give me my money back. Haze, roll up. I need to get high."

"Now you are talking my language."

The weed would help Lucky relax and think of his next move. He knew the mayor was using Atlanta as bait to get him to make a mistake. Truth be told, if they knew where his family was located, they would have taken Tamika and Tasha already. They'd pulled the same stunt in Cape Cod, and Lucky almost fell for the trap. This time, he was going to call Tasha and tell her to bounce. Last time he'd spoken to her, he told her everything would be okay. He was hoping when he called her, she would listen to him and leave.

Within minutes, Haze was already sparking the blunt. Lucky couldn't wait to take a few pulls. He needed to calm his nerves. He took a long, slow drag, exhaled through his mouth and nose, then inhaled the cloud of smoke.

"Damn, Lucky! You have to show me that trick. That was one hell of a pull."

Lucky laughed and took a few more pulls. He knew he heard the mayor say they had his money. For some strange reason, in the back of his head, he felt like the mayor was bluffing. As he passed the blunt, Haze inquired about their next move.

"So, who are we going after now? Are we killing the cops or kidnapping their families? Or are we heading down to Atlanta to get your family and make sure they are safe?"

"I'm not going down to Atlanta. The drive is crazy. I'm just going to call her. I'm pretty sure she already heard the press conference. I know they don't know where she's at in Atlanta. We renting a villa from one of her friends. Nothing is under her name. In fact, they don't even know her name. They're trying to get me to come out there. They tried that in Cape Cod."

"I remember hearing about the Cape Cod shooting on TV."

"They did the same exact thing. They mentioned they were heading to Cape Cod, and I headed out there because I thought they knew where my daughter was staying. They didn't know shit. They just knew they were in Cape Cod but didn't have an address. I just so happened to bump into them first before they bumped into me. That's when I saw them at the post office and took two of them out in broad daylight."

"You are a crazy muthafucka, Lucky."

"Hey, when you trying to defend your family, you do whatever is necessary. Those pricks were going to kill them just to get back at me."

"Do you want me to call your baby mama like last time, or you are going to handle it?"

"I got it. I just hope this doesn't scare her off and she decides to disappear."

"Why would she disappear?"

"She bounced on me before for not changing my act. I know she'll bounce again. She begged me not to come up to New York. Tasha loves me, but she's the definition of a real independent woman. She doesn't need any nigga to be happy."

"Damn! Sounds like my girl."

"Li'l homie, I don't give a fuck about a female's race. White, black, brown, or even fuckin' green, they are all cut the same. At the end of the day, all they want to do is be with you. They would go through whatever to end up with you by their side."

"I see what you saying. That's why my sisters do all the dumb shit they do for their boyfriends."

"I was really sincere about coming back and beginning a new life with her. I even told my daughter things will be different when I return. I don't want my baby mama to take away my last chance of fixing my family."

"She will wait. She's a rider, right?"

"She is. She knew I had to finish my business here first before moving forward. On our last convo, she told me to hurry up and finish so I could go back home."

After smoking two more blunts, Lucky was still hyped. He loved how the mayor was trying to pin it all on him. He wasn't surprised or upset, but he did think the press conference was a nice touch. The mayor made it seem like, for the city to move forward, Lucky had to be captured or eliminated.

Lucky didn't care and wasn't going to run, either. He wanted to go against his own rules because he couldn't wait anymore. He was done with the fucking patience game.

"Damn, Haze! I want to run up in Tuna's house tonight," Lucky said as he cocked back the 9-millimeter lying by the computer desk.

"I'm ready. Let's use those fuckin' pipe bombs." Haze let a cloud of smoke out his mouth, trying to do the trick Lucky did.

"Shit! We have to wait for Blood. We need his help. I can't lie. For the first time ever, I can't be patient. I'm going to take Tasha's advice and quickly finish this mess. As bad as I want to kill those muthafuckas, I need to be smart as well. I'm trying to walk away alive after I'm done. I'm not ready for either box."

"Either box?" a confused Haze asked. "Oh, I get it," he quickly said before Lucky could respond. "You mean jail or a coffin. I got you."

"Exactly, li'l homie. I'm not going to either one."

"Shit! Me either," Haze shouted as he pulled out his gun and cocked it back as well.

As they both were playing wild cowboys, they heard the front door unlock. They both ran toward the door, their guns pointed.

As they got closer, to their surprise, it was a sexy brown-skinned babe about five-five, with long, silky black hair down to her big ass. Her beauty and booty threw Haze off. He lowered his gun and mumbled, "Damn!"

Lucky quickly grabbed the unidentified female by the mouth and neck as Haze closed the door. He threw her on the floor and pointed his gun at her. "Listen, we don't want to hurt you, but if you scream, I'm going to shoot you. Are we clear?"

"Yes," the terrified girl replied.

"Is this your apartment?"

"Yes," she mumbled, tears coming down her face.

"We both know Blood. He said we could stay here. He told us you were away handling business. Where were you at again?" Lucky asked her. He remembered Blood said she was in Atlanta. If she lied, he was going to put a bullet right through her head.

"I was in Atlanta. Where is Blood? I need his new number. I been trying to reach him for a few days now." The young lady felt a lot more comfortable when they mentioned her boyfriend's name. "Can I please get off the floor?" she asked.

"Yes, my bad. We had to make sure first." Lucky lowered his gun and helped her up. "What's your name, sweetie?"

"My name is Krystal. And you two? Y'all look like a father-and-son team."

"Oh, you got jokes. Don't make me put my gun back in your mouth. My name is Rick, and that's Chris."

"So who are you guys? The ones who pulled off the storage hit?"

"We don't discuss business." Lucky walked behind Krystal and hit her with the back of his gun, and she passed out from the unexpected blow.

After she dropped to the floor, Haze took a few steps back. He was also taken by surprise. "What the fuck, Lucky! I thought that was Blood's girl."

"Didn't you hear what the fuck she said? Are you paying attention? The bitch just said you guys are the ones from the storage hit. Whose fuckin' storage just got hit?"

Haze was upset at himself for not picking up on that. "My bad. That slipped by me."

"Ever since the bitch walked in, you been mesmerized. Don't think I didn't notice when you lowered your gun earlier. Don't let her beauty trick you, li'l homie. If you ever live by any of the codes, live by that one—always stay focused. Look for something so we can tie this bitch up and wait for her to wake up."

As Haze looked around for rope, Lucky was staring at Krystal. He was wondering why the pretty young lady decided to come back to the apartment. He started checking her for wires to see if she was an informant. He didn't find any wires or weapons. He started to feel bad for knocking such a sexy thing out.

Haze found some rope and two pairs of handcuffs in the closet.

"Damn! Shorty's a freak," Lucky shouted, and they both laughed.

Lucky went to the dining room and grabbed a chair. They both picked up Krystal and sat her up. They handcuffed her hands behind the back of the chair and tied the rest of her body with sheets. As they attempted to stuff a sock in her mouth, she started gaining consciousness.

"Lucky, she's waking up."

"I see," Lucky said as he finally got the sock in. "Welcome back, bitch."

By the time Krystal realized what happened, it was too late. She was already tied up. She knew she shouldn't have tried that joke about the father-and-son team.

As Lucky and Haze were both looking at her like prey, she quickly realized they didn't give a fuck about Blood. Lucky pointed his gun near her eye. The barrel was so close, she could actually see the slug. She began to cry and tried to yell, but the sock was too deep in her mouth.

"Again, I'm going to ask you a few questions. When I remove the sock, all I want to hear is the answer. If you scream or attempt anything, we will kill you. It's your choice—live with a bump on the back of your head, or die. Are we clear?" Lucky said in a slow but deadly tone.

Krystal could feel through his voice that he wasn't joking. She started nodding her head up and down.

"Okay, you asked if we were part of the team that hit the storage. Do you know which storage they hit?" Lucky removed the sock.

"I don't know the name," Krystal said. "But it was in the Bronx. Blood's childhood friend worked there. His name is, well, was Divine. He was killed along with

Blood's brother, Pee-wee. I swear, I don't know the name of the place."

Lucky paused. Krystal just fucked his head up by mentioning Divine's name. He couldn't believe Divine was behind it as well, because the night of the shooting, Lucky personally went in the safe room to grab the big guns. He saw all the money there, unless Blood still carried out the plan after the shooting and fire. Divine gave him the code, so he must have gone in and cleaned house.

"That sneaky muthafucka. I see why he's flossing so much money. What else you know?"

"That's pretty much it. I know after his brother and Divine were killed, he carried the plan out with new help. I thought it was you guys who helped him."

"I'm actually the guy they robbed. Where is the rest of my money?"

"I don't know."

"That bitch is lying, boss!" Haze yelled. He thought he'd been standing on the sideline for too long and just wanted to get in on the action.

"I know. I'm going to give her five seconds to rethink her answer." Lucky slowly screwed in the silencer.

"I swear, I don't know about the money. I'm not allowed to ask about his business. I just spend the money he gives me."

"You just spend the money, huh? Let me paint the picture I see. You are his bottom bitch, his main squeeze. He trusts you with his money. I'm sure you know more than what you are telling us. You could help us find the rest of the money. Your five seconds is up."

As soon as Lucky tried to stuff the sock back in her mouth, Krystal said, "Wait. How do I know my safety is guaranteed? You still might kill me."

"Are you willing to risk it and find out if I'm bluffing?"

Krystal thought about her options for a few seconds and quickly started running her mouth to save her ass. "Okay, there's about another eight hundred thousand dollars in the bedroom. It's stuffed in the closet behind a fake wall Blood built. The only way in is to break the wall down."

"You better not be lying, bitch." Lucky turned to Haze. "Go check out the wall in the closet and see if she's telling the truth." He turned back to Krystal. "Okay, there's still a lot of money missing, so where is it?"

"I have at least three hundred thousand that's under the mattress, inside the box spring, but that's about it. Where he stashed the rest of the money, I'm clueless. I know he has other bitches on the side, but I don't know where the rest of the money is."

Lucky believed her and lowered his gun. He put the sock back in her mouth and covered her face with a pillowcase. He went and helped Haze break the wall.

Krystal was telling the truth. There were two duffel bags filled with money and a few pieces of jewelry as well.

"Are we taking the ice as well, Lucky?"

"Hell yeah. We taking everything. You could keep the ice."

"For real. That's what's up."

As Haze was packing away the jewelry, Lucky was ripping up the box spring. Krystal again was telling the truth.

Haze removed the money and packed it with the rest. In total, they now had about 1.1 million dollars, enough money to bounce and start a new life.

"Damn, Lucky! Don't we have enough to—"

"Don't say it. I know what you about to say. Let's stay focused. I know never in your life have you touched so much money before. Don't let it poison your mind. We just need to wait for Blood to call."

"That's what I wanted to ask you. How we going to lure Blood in here?"

"I got it. I will wait until he calls me. Trust me, he will show up."

"What about all this money? We can't leave it here."

"You're right. Take both bags to your car and lock them in the trunk."

"Bet."

"Wait. There's like over a hundred and fifty thousand in the safe. Take that shit, too."

"What about all the guns?" Haze asked.

"Take some of them, but grab all the bullets you can. Once we kill Blood, we'll rent a room till we take care of our business."

"What about Krystal?"

"Collateral damage, li'l homie."

"We killing her?" a shocked Haze asked.

"Don't forget, she knows how you look. She saw your face. Right now, the media is just after me. Let's keep it that way."

"You're right. Fuck it then! The bitch has to die."

As Haze packed up the rest of the money and guns, Lucky walked back over to Krystal and removed the pillowcase.

"Sweetie, you said you didn't get in contact with Blood, right? So far, you been telling the truth, so don't fuck up."

Krystal nodded yes.

"Well, I'm going to have to leave you tied up for a few more hours before I let you go. I'm sorry we had to meet under these circumstances. You seem like a nice lady. You just fell in love with the wrong guy. I'm going to cover your face up again. It's better you don't see what we're doing."

Lucky placed the pillowcase back over her face and waited for Haze to come back. It was going on ten minutes, and Haze hadn't returned from the car. Lucky thought the worst. Maybe Haze jumped in the car and bounced on him.

As Lucky began to get worried, in came Haze through the door.

"It took you long enough."

"I was moving the car. I parked it down the block. Here are the keys." Haze threw the keys to Lucky.

"Good idea. Watch this bitch while I go in the room and call Tasha. I'm going to be a minute. If anybody comes to the door, empty your clip on their ass."

"I got you," Haze replied.

"I'm not playing. I don't care who it is. Start blasting."

Chapter 11

Another Harlem Shooting

Lucky went in the room and dialed Tasha's number, and she picked up on the first ring.

"Tasha, it's me."

"I know. Are you ready to come home now?"

"Did you see the mayor's conference?" Lucky asked, ignoring her question.

"You know I did. What you want me to do?"

Lucky paused. The last thing he expected to hear was Tasha was still willing to follow suit. "Well, I first called to make sure you were okay. I know hearing the mayor mention Atlanta had you nervous."

"I knew he was bluffing. They just knew you were down here, but I knew he was bullshitting. No one knows we moved down here except my friend, and she doesn't know who you are."

"That's my baby girl. That's why I love you. Listen, I'm almost done, but every time I turn around, there's something new involved. I should be ready within the next day or so."

"For real. Are you serious?"

"I'm positive, but we can't stay in Atlanta. In fact, I want you to leave today if possible."

"Okay, we could go to either Florida or Arizona. We have relatives in both states."

"Let's go with Arizona. We could keep a lower profile in there. I will call you back in a day or so and get the address. Tasha, you have to bounce quickly. The mayor may be bluffing, but I'm not taking any risk."

"Okay, I will. Hold on. Your daughter wants to speak to you."

Lucky's heart paused. He hadn't spoken to Tamika since leaving Atlanta a few days ago.

"Hello, Daddy. You there?"

"Hey, sugar. How are you?" Lucky said, his voice cracking.

"I'm fine. When are you coming home? I miss you."

"I will be home soon, sugar."

"Remember, you promised you would. Mommy has been crying a lot. I know why. She thinks you are not coming back."

"Mommy just likes to worry a lot. Daddy will be home. I can't lose any more time apart from you. You keep your mommy strong till I get there. I love you, and I will see you soon."

"Okay, Daddy, hurry up. I want to go to the mall. I love you. Good night. I'm going to give the phone back to Mommy."

"Hello. Baby, are you still there?" Tasha asked quickly, hoping Lucky didn't hang up the phone.

"I'm here."

"So, you will call me?"

"Yeah, I will hit you. Remember, start packing."

"I got it, baby, whatever you say. I'm sorry I was tripping last time we spoke. I was out of line. I know why you are doing it. I shouldn't add any stress. You need my support. I love you, be safe, and get those muthafuckas, baby."

"Ha! That's the support I want to hear, baby. I gotta go. I will see you soon. Remember what I taught you—stay on point."

"Always. *Mwa!* Love ya!"

Lucky sat on the edge of the bed and took a few deep breaths. Hearing Tamika's voice took him through a ride of emotions. It was critical now that every step going forward be mistake free. Everything was on the line.

As Lucky got up to walk out the room, his cell phone started ringing. He turned back around. He thought maybe it was Tasha calling back, until he saw the number on the caller ID.

"Yo, who's this?"

"It's Blood. What's good? I'm going to stop by there, lay low for a day or two, then I'm bouncing out of town."

"When are you coming? It's going on eight o'clock."

"I should be over there in, like, thirty minutes."

"See you then." Lucky was relieved. He didn't even have to lure Blood in.

He opened the door and called Haze in.

"What's up, boss? Everything all right with the family?"

"Yeah, they're good. Listen, Blood just called. He said he's like half hour away."

"Damn! We need to get ready, then."

"I know. I need you to load up and wait outside for him."

"Outside in the streets? Are you sure?"

"Yeah, man. I just want you to watch him and make sure he enters the building. I want you to look around and make sure he's alone. Once you see him get in the elevator, hit me on the radio, then run up the stairs. But don't let him see you. Stay low. I'll be waiting for him in the hallway. Once the elevator doors open, the first thing he will see is this big-ass gun. If he makes a move, I'm going to light his ass up."

"Okay, I'm going to get ready. What about the bimbo sitting in the living room?"

"One to the head."

Haze walked out and started loading up the guns and threw on his black hoodie. Before Haze went downstairs, Lucky passed him a two-way radio. That way they could communicate instantly. He went downstairs and waited, like Lucky instructed.

Lucky grabbed the bulletproof vest and the 12-gauge shotgun. He wanted to blow Blood's face away.

As they both waited, Haze hit him up on the radio. "I think I see him. He's getting out a car from almost two blocks down."

"So how you could tell it's him?"

"It's just a feeling. I'm going to get a closer look to see if that's him."

"Be careful."

"Copy." Haze felt this was the perfect moment to prove to Lucky he was a real thug.

Haze was correct. It was Blood getting out of a cab down the street. Blood always played every situation safe, just like Lucky. He knew the cops and feds were looking for him. As Blood got closer to the building, he noticed something, so he stopped.

Haze was behind him, so he also stopped.

Blood noticed Krystal's white BMW parked in front of the building. That caught him off guard, so when he turned around to look at the car again, he noticed Haze behind him, wearing a hoodie. He didn't waste any time, pulling out quicker than Haze and shooting as he ran for cover.

Haze wasn't as quick as Blood, but he was also able to pull out. Haze let off a few shots, too, and then ran for cover. Haze leaned against a parked car. That was when he realized he was shot twice, in the stomach and right shoulder. There was blood pouring everywhere. From the look of things, Haze could easily bleed to death. Haze was still letting off rounds, though. He figured, if he kept shooting, Blood would never know he was hurt.

Haze was so busy running for cover and attending to his own wounds, he failed to see that Blood was hit as well, on the upper thigh. The shot wasn't life-threatening, but it was enough to keep a good distance between the both of them. Blood slowly was creeping closer to Haze and letting off more shots than him.

Haze felt overmatched and decided to preserve his bullets. He was praying for Lucky to come down and save him. He wasn't ready to go yet. He thought about his pregnant girlfriend and unborn child. Now it was looking like a big mistake coming up to New York to help Lucky.

All that gangster tough talk was no longer in his vocabulary. He finally realized he wasn't built for this part of the game. He realized what every other wannabe killer realized—bullets did hurt, and burned like hell.

As Haze sat behind a parked car, bullets were still flying past his ears, the shots getting closer and closer.

When Blood paused to reload his .40 Glock, Lucky sneaked up behind him and blew a hole in the back of his head. His body slammed against the concrete, and brain fragments splattered everywhere. A close-range shotgun blast would disfigure any body parts. Lucky didn't even get a chance to ask Blood why or where the rest of the money was. He just knew his li'l homie was in trouble and he had to help him.

Lucky ran over to aid Haze, but it was too late. Blood had shot him two more times. One shot caught him in the back of the head and came out his left eye. Lucky almost fainted when he saw Haze's lifeless body lying in between two parked cars. When he heard sirens in the background, he ran down the block and spotted Haze's car. He jumped in and sped off.

Lucky had tears coming down his face as he was driving, not knowing where to go. He knew he endangered Haze's life by inviting him to help him out. He just didn't think anything would happen to the young buck. All Haze wanted to do was prove himself to Lucky. That was a hard burden to carry.

As he was driving around Harlem, he decided to head over to the Bronx. With Haze and Blood gone, Lucky was back to square one, no help on his side.

Lucky was driving around, trying to find a place to lay his head for a day or two. After driving for about a good forty-five minutes, he decided to drive to the Capri. The Capri was listed as a hotel but was basically a fuck station. They were one of the only hotels/motels with a bar inside with hookers waiting to provide all kind of freaky shit. You needed an ID to rent a room, but Lucky also knew that the owner was a low-down, dirty hustler. He figured he would just approach the bulletproof window and slip them five hundred dollars.

When he arrived at the hotel, he was a bit hesitant. He didn't want to risk his face being exposed. He pulled up to the parking lot, where the hotel's front desk manager was having a smoke.

Lucky approached him. "Hey, do you work here? Because I have a question."

"I'm the manager on duty. How can I help you, my friend?"

"Listen, I want to rent a room for the night, but I don't have any ID on me."

"I'm sorry, I can't help you, and we need ID, just in case something happens in the room."

"Here is five hundred dollars. All I need is room keys. I'm not interested in tearing up the hotel room. I just need some sleep."

"Are you joking, sir?"

"I'm not joking. Take the money. Go inside and bring me out a set of keys."

"Okay, give me, like, five minutes."

Lucky was glad to hear the manager was willing to accept the five hundred, which was more than his weekly paycheck. As Lucky waited, two sexy females dressed like strippers were leaving the hotel, mad as hell. Lucky quickly stopped them and asked what was wrong.

Only one of the girls stopped. The other jumped in the waiting cab.

"This nasty old man upstairs was supposed to pay us to have sex with him, but once we get to his room, the old bastard said he only had enough to pay for one girl. We left five seconds after he said that dumb shit."

"Damn! That's fucked up. Don't leave just yet. I'm checking in myself."

"Are you alone?" she asked as she got closer and placed her hand on his dick.

"Yeah, I'm alone. I'm just waiting for a new set of keys."

"You *are* checking in alone. Do you need some company, daddy?" the girl said, hoping Lucky had enough money to keep her pretty ass in his room. "What's your name, daddy?" She let go of his balls and wrapped her hand around his dick.

"My name is Larry. I would love some company. How much is it going to cost me?"

"Well, my name is Princess. I will give you a special price. If you just want head, it will be one hundred dollars, but if you want to fuck and do it all, and I mean whatever you want, daddy, it will run two hundred."

"That's it. Two hundred? You better tell your friend to go ahead and leave, because you are staying with me for the night, Princess."

"I sure will, daddy."

As the girl went to tell her friend that she could leave, the manager came out with his set of keys. The girl returned and asked if her friend could join them in the room.

Within seconds, Lucky had a change of heart. "You know what, baby girl? I'm sorry to have wasted your time. Here's a hundred dollars for your trouble. I changed my mind. I need to spend this night alone."

"Damn, daddy, you are a big balla. Niggas don't give bitches a C-note for no reason. Let me come upstairs and make you feel happy. My girl and I will suck the head off your dick."

"Sounds lovely, but after the night I had, the last thing on my mind is pussy. I could go home for that. I just want to spend the night alone. I'm good, baby. You have yourself a good night," Lucky said as he went in the hotel.

Princess felt hurt by Lucky's rejection. She stood there for a second after he went in the hotel, hoping he would come out and say he was just joking. That never happened. She jumped in the cab and went about her business.

Lucky sat on the old chair in the room and finally had a moment to mourn Haze's death. It brought more tears to his eyes. He really broke down when he remembered he had an unborn child. He felt like it was his fault, even though the young buck had his mind made up, ready to die, and no one could change his mind. Lucky knew the risk, but it was still a shocker. Haze had so much to look forward to.

Lucky felt like his luck was running out. Everyone around him either died or betrayed him. It only meant his fate was looming and getting close. He was just hoping that it had a happy ending.

He'd accomplished what he wanted, which was to kill Blood. He was upset that he didn't get a chance to get some info out of him first. That police in him always thought about an interrogation first. A tied-up Blood with guns in his face would have talked. Lucky had witnessed the hardest thugs snitch for nothing and would have loved the chance to speak to him under duress.

Lucky was down on himself, but he wasn't going to lose sleep over it. He did feel bad for shooting Krystal, but it had to be done. He didn't have second thoughts when he shot her. That was who he was and would always be, a natural at it. It didn't matter what he did, he always wanted to be the best. So, once he crossed the line and started killing, his feelings went numb.

Lucky knew in his heart he could change and start a new life. He was just hoping it wasn't too late. He had that one relapse episode at Sergio's house, but ever since that night he hadn't had any cocaine calls. He knew he had his addiction under control. Well, at least, he felt like he did. As long as his life was drama free about his past, he would be okay.

He wiped his tears and realized he had to come up with new strategies. He'd just lost two individuals who were going to help him take down Captain Tuna, Speedy, and the mayor. Leaving town was starting to make more sense to Lucky. If he quit, he would walk away with over a million dollars, 1.3 to be exact, enough to give it a big consideration.

By killing Blood, he eliminated any chance of finding the rest of the money. He was puzzled and helpless. He couldn't pull the job off alone. He had to pick one target out of Tuna, Speedy, and the mayor. It was really between Tuna and the mayor. Lucky hated both of them with a passion.

He decided to take out Tuna. He could live with Speedy and the mayor staying alive. Hopefully, they each would serve long prison terms, but Tuna, he wanted him dead.

He jumped in the bed and turned on the TV to get his mind off his li'l homie. The news was already reporting the shooting that took place that left three dead, including a female who was killed execution-style. Lucky was surprised his name wasn't mentioned as a lead suspect. He figured his name would pop up after they checked the apartment for fingerprints. "I should have burned that building down," he said to himself.

He turned the TV off and just lay there. He put his hand in his pants and began rubbing his balls. He smacked himself over the head for turning down Princess and her friend.

He ended up dozing off. He needed the rest. Tomorrow was going to be judgment day. The day it came to an end.

The mayor was tossing and turning when his phone started ringing around midnight. "Hello."

"I'm sorry to bother you, sir. My name is Anita Flowers, police spokesperson. We can't get hold of Richard Claiborne. We have a problem, sir."

"What's going on?" the mayor said as he got up and off the bed.

"There's been another big shoot out in Harlem today. We have fatalities."

"Please, don't tell me there were police officers."

"No, sir, they were civilians, two males and a female. The female was found tied up with a single gunshot wound to the head."

"Oh my God! We have any leads?"

"The identities of the two males have been confirmed. One of them is Daquan 'Blood' Mooks. He was a person of interest in the shooting that left three FBI agents dead."

"I'm aware of the first victim. He was second on the most wanted list, behind Lucky. What about the other suspect?"

"According to the ID we found in his wallet, he's from Glen Burnie, Maryland. His name is Dante Jones. He has a felony conviction on his record, two years in jail for drug charges. He'd been on parole ever since. We still don't have a connection as to why he's up here. However, after running fingerprint checks in the apartment where the female was found, we have confirmed Lucky was in the apartment. In fact, his fingerprints were all over the dead female."

"We are positive those were Lucky's prints?" a skeptical mayor asked.

"Yes, we are," a confident Anita answered.

"That explains why the other victim from Maryland was up here. He must have helped Lucky come back to New York."

"Do you want me to follow up with Richard? Who do I contact if I can't reach Richard again?"

"No, I'm afraid Richard is on leave for a few months, until further notice. Please call me and keep me up to date. I have to call the governor and then face the media."

"Is there anything you need from me?"

"How good are you with handling the media?"

"With all due respect, Your Honor, I'm the one who's been thrown on the front line to speak to the media on behalf of the department. It's no secret these past few months have been historically challenging."

"Ms. Flowers, if you could step in and take the lead on the investigation, it would be greatly appreciated. You will get complete clearance. Are you up for it?"

"Yes, I am, sir. Thank you."

"I can't offer you Richard's job, because my term is currently in jeopardy. But I will make sure you receive nothing but the highest recommendations, and secure you a slot with the next mayor as their spokesperson."

"Again, thank you, sir. I will give you a call as soon as I receive any updates."

The mayor felt confident Anita would be able to handle the situation. Even though he had been half awake and couldn't sleep, he really wished he hadn't picked up the call. Last thing he wanted to hear was, 'More dead bodies. He wanted to jump back in bed and act like the call never happened.'

Chapter 12

Tuna, the Last Catch

Around seven in the morning, Lucky finally woke up. For a second he was hoping when he opened his eyes, he was back with Tasha and Tamika. After snapping out of his fantasy dream, he jumped out of bed and turned on the TV. While he waited for the news to come on, all he was concerned with was taking care of Tuna. After he was done with Tuna, he would go down to Arkansas and handle Diamond.

It was time to start putting together the plan to catch Tuna slipping. He was an easy target, so Lucky knew exactly where to find him. As Lucky was going over the details, the TV caught his attention when Destine Diaz's live report came on. He stopped what he was doing and sat back up on the edge of the bed.

"Hello, New York. I'm back with more news and dead bodies in Harlem. Well, first I want to let everyone know about the dead body in the Bronx. This body may be connected to Lucky. According to police officers at the scene, they found Sergio Martinez tortured to death. According to the police, fingerprints taken from the scene match Lucky's.

"Then, in Harlem this morning, three more bodies popped up. We have two male suspects found shot to death outside in the streets. There was also a female found tied up and killed execution-style with a single

shot to the back of the head. This shooting happened right in the middle of the upscale Riverside neighborhood of Harlem.

"The two dead males have been confirmed as Dante 'Haze' Jones from Glen Burnie, Maryland, and Daquan 'Blood' Mooks from Harlem. Details about Dante's identity are still sketchy, but investigators believe he's connected with Lucky. After Lucky's shooting at the Holiday Inn, he disappeared in the Glen Burnie area. The police are trying to determine if Dante was the one who assisted Lucky while he was down in Maryland. One of our sources has confirmed that the Arundel County Police Department in Maryland is working with the NYPD in conducting a proper background check on the suspect.

"Now, here is where it gets interesting. The other suspect, Daquan Mooks, is the other half of the deadly Mooks brothers, known for pulling off memorable crimes. These brothers have terrorized the Harlem community for years, killing people for money and sometimes fun. They were charged but never convicted of many crimes, including a diamond heist, armored truck jobs, and suspected involvement in Lucky's underground operation as the cleanup team. Everyone always wondered why they were roaming the streets as free men.

"Daquan's brother, Dwayne, was burned alive in that shooting in the storage facility owned and operated by Lucky. Daquan 'Blood' Mooks was on New York's most wanted list. He was a suspect in the shooting that left three FBI agents dead the other day in Harlem. Investigators are trying to figure out what took place. If both Dante and Daquan were working with Lucky, how come they are dead and he's not? Did Lucky pull the trigger on his own team, or did someone else come to kill them and Lucky got away? Police

believe the mysterious girl found shot in the head may be Lucky's girl. They say his fingerprints are all over her body. It looks like detectives will have their hands full.

"I've lost count of the amount of murders since Perry's trial began, but there's been nonstop warfare, which looks like it won't end until all parties kill each other. This is Destine Diaz, from Channel Five."

Lucky sat there with a smirk on his face because they'd found Sergio's corpse, but something didn't make sense. He and Blood had wiped everything down at Sergio's apartment. If the police found prints, then the CIA must have made that happen, to make the public aware that he was responsible for all the killings.

Lucky needed to make his move. Checkout was in a few hours, and he needed a new car. Haze's car was too hot to drive. He ran outside and cleaned everything out of the car.

On his way back to the room, he noticed a cab dropping off a couple. He walked up to the driver's side. "Hey, I need a ride to 125th Street and Lexington Avenue."

"Twenty-five," the African cabdriver said.

"I just have to check out. Give me five minutes, and I will give you forty dollars."

"Thank you. I wait here. Hurry please. Thank you."

The mayor was down the street from Tuna's house. Tuna was waiting outside and got in the car when it pulled up.

"What the fuck took so long to get me out?" Tuna said before he sat down.

"Things have changed a bit, especially after the commissioner was killed."

"That's bullshit! But fuck it. Anyway, what's up? I know there's only one reason why you muthafuckas bailed me out. You need help with Lucky."

"You right. We need your help. He's kicking our asses bad," the mayor said.

"Well, we'll see, because I have a perfect plan to get him out of hiding."

That wasn't what the mayor wanted to hear. "Listen, I just need you to lay low for at least three days. You have to stay away from the public's eye."

"I can't stay here for three days straight."

"Okay, well, maybe two days, but I need you out of the spotlight. We don't have the power like we used to. The federal government is about to take over the whole police department's daily operations. We need to catch Lucky and return things back to normal."

"What about my situation? We already are going to do heavy time for shooting that black boy," Tuna said.

"If we capture Lucky, the CIA is going to help us flip everything back on him. Most of those charges will be dropped."

"What about the Perry case?" Tuna asked with a look of desperation. "I can't get a lower sentence?"

"There's nothing we could do about the Perry Coleman case. I'm sorry."

"So I'm just supposed to accept a nine-to-life bid. That's nine years, Your Honor."

They continued to talk for about fifteen minutes. The mayor could only hope that Tuna followed his instruction to lay low.

After the mayor left, Tuna said to himself, "Shit! Stay here for three days straight? Never." He pulled out his cell phone and called up the Candy Shop. He told Dimples to have a girl at his spot on 102nd Street in about three hours.

Tuna wasn't about to stay confined in his own home. He broke off his ankle bracelet, kissed his wife, and left. He worked for the commissioner, not the mayor. He knew he was going back to jail, so he was going out with a bang.

Meanwhile, the mayor was driving with a smile on his face. All he needed was for Tuna to stay put in the house. The mayor was on his way to Speedy's house. He knew Speedy wouldn't mind staying home.

When the mayor arrived, Speedy invited him in. The mayor told him his plans about capturing Lucky.

"No disrespect, I'm not interested in doing nothing else but spending time with my family until I go back to prison."

"You can't turn your back on us now," the mayor said in a low, disappointed tone.

"There is no *us*. I finally figured it all out. These last few days of confinement have cleared my head."

"Well, it's your decision, but if we capture Lucky, a lot of those charges will get dropped, and you would be able to spend more time with your family."

"I don't care about the charges we have pending. I'm more interested in the one I pleaded guilty to. I already made thousand of mistakes. I don't need to add any more. My time is valuable, and I need to spend it with family, not chasing a rat. I'm done."

The mayor realized Speedy was sincere about his commitment to staying home until his next court date. That was all he wanted, but he had to make it at least seem like he was disappointed in his actions.

"Okay, I see I wasted my time coming out here. I could have just called you. Remember who made it possible for you to come out and spend this precious time with your family. You dwell on that. You know how to contact us," the mayor said as he walked toward the front door.

Speedy didn't respond to the mayor's last comment. He didn't even make eye contact with him. Speedy knew the mayor was right, which made him question his decision. Speedy was raised in a household filled with cops. In fact, both his parents were detectives. One thing he'd learned from birth was the code of honor among the blue. He had to make a decision. He didn't know if he should stay home with his family or join his work family, which was all he had known for the last fifteen years.

The mayor called the governor to give an update.

"I just finished visiting both Tuna and Speedy," he said. "And the plan is in motion. They're both going to be in their house for at least the next forty-eight hours. We need to set up surveillance teams on both locations ASAP."

"I'm on it. What kind of manpower we need?"

"Well, judging from our luck, we need as much as we can get at both locations. But make sure they are our veteran team. Lucky will spot them from a mile away if they're not careful. We can't fuck this one up," the mayor said. "This is our last chance."

"Understood. I will start making calls as soon as we get off the phone. Are you on your way back to the city?"

"Yes, I'm on the Long Island Expressway right now. Call me, once the team is set up. We need to post up within hours, if possible."

"Got it," the governor said.

Chapter 13

The Final Stakeout

It was going on four o'clock in the afternoon, and the surveillance team was intact. A team of twelve staked out Tuna's house because they felt confident Lucky would attack there first, while a team of four staked out Speedy's.

The mayor checked in with his surveillance team. He radioed his lead agent, Captain Mark Schuler, who was watching Tuna's house.

"Captain, come in. What's the latest?"

"It looks like he's not home, sir. We been here for almost two hours, and so far there are still no signs of Tuna."

"Damn! I don't know why he couldn't just follow simple directions. What about Speedy? What's the update?"

"Speedy's car is parked in the driveway. His wife and kids are running all over the house, but still no visual on him, either. He was last seen about forty-five minutes ago. We believe he's actually sleeping, sir."

"What about their ankle bracelets?" the mayor asked.

"They are indicating that they are both home. That's why we are confused. We are certain Tuna isn't home. We been outside his house, and there is still no sign of him."

"They must know how to tamper with the devices. Okay, Captain, please have your eyes open for Lucky. He doesn't know they're not home. Remember, he's a former detective. He will do what any other cop would do—stake the place out first. Hit me as soon as you have visual contact. Remember, shoot first as soon as you have contact."

"Affirmative."

The mayor was disappointed to hear Tuna wasn't home and that Speedy wasn't willing to cooperate, especially after speaking to both of them earlier in the day. It was delaying his plan to capture Lucky.

The mayor was becoming nervous again. He was starting to feel like it was his last day on earth. He was glad he'd spent a great night at home with his family. He didn't jump the gun and call the governor, figuring the best plan at the moment was to be patient and wait for Lucky to show.

Captain Schuler radioed in. "Sir, come in."

"Tell me some good news, Captain."

"Speedy is on the move, sir."

"Stay on him and keep me updated turn by turn."

Five minutes later, Captain Schuler reported, "It looks like he's heading toward the Triboro Bridge."

"He's coming to Harlem, maybe to meet up with Tuna. I know they had a secret spot somewhere in Spanish Harlem. I don't know the address. Stay on him, Captain, and please don't get made. Speedy was part of an elite team of officers as well. They were the best in their field."

"We understand, sir."

Captain Tuna pulled up to his old hangout spot on 102nd Street and Lexington Avenue and saw a yellow cab sitting in front. He rolled up next to it, his gun on his lap. He saw a female in the cab. That was when it hit him. She was one of the girls from the escort service, the Candy Shop.

He lowered his window. “Candy Shop!” he hollered.

“Yes, my name is Mindy. Are you the sexy Tuna guy all the girls talk about? You late, pretty boy.”

“Listen, let yourself in the building. Let me park, and I will be right back.”

As Mindy paid the cab and got out, Tuna drove around the block a few times to make sure no one was following him. He knew Lucky knew about the apartment, so he wanted to be extra careful.

After about ten minutes, Tuna finally made it in the building. “I’m sorry, baby. Parking is hard to find around here.”

“I was starting to wonder if maybe I scared you off.”

“I wouldn’t leave something as pretty as you stranded. I haven’t been in this apartment in a few days. I’m hoping everything is still intact.”

“As long as you have the money, baby, I don’t care where we fuck.” Mindy grabbed Tuna’s dick.

As Mindy and Tuna walked up the steps, Speedy was pulling up on the old hangout spot. He knew Tuna had to be up there. His plan was to see what Tuna’s intentions were. If he felt like Tuna was going to turn into a rat, he was going to kill him, then kill himself. But if Tuna was okay with him falling back on this last push for Lucky, then he would just walk away and go home.

Speedy was tired of all the bullshit. He wanted to find a quick resolution. He parked and started walking toward the building. He looked down the street and waved at the surveillance car that was following him.

***

"Sir, come in."

"Yes, Captain. Where did he stop?" the mayor asked.

"He just entered a building on 102nd Street and Lexington Avenue."

"Okay, I'm dispatching additional help. Stay put and out of sight until more help arrives."

"He already made us. Right before he entered the building, he waved at us."

"Well, still stay put and out of sight," an angry mayor said. "Didn't I warn you to be careful? Never mind. Don't do anything until help arrives."

"Affirmative."

As Tuna tried to open the front door, Mindy couldn't wait until they entered the apartment. She started kissing him all over him. She wanted to fuck him in the hallway.

"Calm down, baby girl. Let me open the door first."

As Tuna swung open the front door, Lucky was standing there waiting, pointing the same 12-gauge he used to blow Blood's head off.

"What the fuck!" were the last words Tuna said as he looked right into Lucky's eye.

Lucky shot him in the chest and watched his body slam against the hallway wall. Mindy began screaming and ran downstairs as fast as she could.

Speedy grabbed her right before she ran out the front door and covered her mouth.

"Sshhh! Calm down! Please, calm down. I'm a police officer. I heard the shot. What's going on? Who's up there? What happened?" Speedy removed his hand from her mouth.

Mindy yelled hysterically, "He shot him! He shot him!"

"Who did?"

"A black guy shot him as soon as he opened the door. Tuna is dead. A black guy shot him."

Speedy released the girl and raced up the flight of steps in time to see Lucky standing over a barely breathing Tuna.

Lucky placed the barrel in Tuna's mouth. "You racist muthafucka! I told you I would kill you." He pulled the trigger and watched part of his face smear all over the wall. As Lucky was about to shoot him again, he was met with about four shots from Speedy's 9-millimeter.

Lucky ducked while letting off two shotgun blasts and dropping the gun on the floor. As he ran in the apartment for cover, he pulled out two 9-millimeters of his own and let off about another twelve shots toward the front door, keeping Speedy at bay.

As Speedy and Lucky were facing off on the third floor, Captain Shuler was on the radio, calling the mayor.

"Shots fired, sir! Shots fired!" the captain yelled.

"Secure the perimeter. Help is minutes away."

The mayor quickly called the governor and told him, "We got him!"

"Where?"

"He's in Spanish Harlem, 102nd Street and Lexington Avenue. He's trapped inside, we believe, with Tuna and Speedy. They are currently in a shoot-out as we speak."

"We'll dispatch the entire department to 102nd Street. He can't get away this time."

"I'm a step ahead of you," the mayor said. "I already made the call. I'm also on my way there."

"I'm on my way as well."

About twenty minutes later, the mayor had the entire block shut down. He had about a hundred police officers and about thirty SWAT members posted all in front of the building.

And news reporters were all over the scene, which was being broadcast live. The potential shooting and hostage situation involving Tuna, Speedy, and Lucky caught the attention of the city, which, once again, was glued to the TV, and watching in anticipation.

The negotiating team at hand attempted to communicate through a bullhorn. They were only going to give them another five minutes before entering and shooting everyone.

As the countdown was nearing its end, the mayor was getting anxious. He was hoping it didn't lead to them having to rush in. He was afraid of what the death toll might be. Lucky could be waiting inside, plucking them off one by one.

With one minute left, an officer yelled, "I see someone coming out!"

Everyone got in their firing positions, and snipers were locked and ready. No one knew what to expect, and out came a suspect dressed in all black, wearing a black mask and waving two guns.

As soon as the mayor saw he was armed, he yelled, "Fire!" and ran for cover.

The gun party began. Snipers hit him first, and then a few officers also discharged their weapons. The suspect's body dropped like rain while shots were still being fired. They rushed toward the suspect and quickly became confused. The handguns were taped around his hands. They removed the mask and noticed it was Detective Speedy.

Lucky had duct-taped his mouth and hands, pushed him out the door, and had run for his escape. And since no one could hear Speedy beg for his life, he was murdered. Once again Lucky embarrassed the police department nationally.

Before the cops had arrived, Speedy ran out of bullets in his standoff with Lucky. Once he noticed he was out of ammo, he gave up, tired of fighting and playing the villain role. If he had had an extra bullet, he would have shot himself.

The second Lucky got ahold of him, he heard the sirens outside. That was the only thing that stopped him from killing Speedy's snake ass. He handcuffed Speedy to the stair rail in the hallway while he ran toward the nearest window.

Lucky couldn't believe the amount of cops outside. With that monkey wrench thrown in his plans, he needed to think fast. He looked over at Speedy and decided to use him to buy him time to escape through the roof.

Right after Lucky pushed Speedy to his death, he turned to run toward the roof, but he noticed a door that led to the back. He decided to skip the roof idea because, knowing the mayor, snipers would be on the roof. He had a better chance of escaping by staying low and out of sight. He didn't have time to map out the area. He was going to have to improvise as he went.

It turned out it was a good decision. The back door led to a small, junky backyard with a bunch of broken refrigerators and air conditioners. Lucky made his way through it. He even had to avoid a few cat-sized rats in the process. He jumped the fence and entered the back of another building and came out on 103rd Street. When he got outside, there were still cops flying past him on their way to 102nd Street. No one noticed him as he calmly walked down the street, his backpack filled with over a million dollars.

Meanwhile, police officers swamped the building, desperately searching for Lucky. Instead, they found the dead body of Captain Tuna, his face on the wall.

When the mayor heard about Tuna's death, he dropped to one knee. It was a wrap. Everything he hoped for went down the drain. A few officers helped the mayor back on his feet. They didn't know what happened.

The mayor refused medical attention, and his staff led him back to his awaiting truck. While the mayor sat there and tried to gain his composure, the lead agent in charge reported back to him.

"Sir, we have searched the entire building, and there are no signs of another suspect."

"Listen, Detective Speedy didn't tie those guns to his hands himself. I want your team to search the building again. Are we clear? As a matter of fact, search every fuckin' building in Spanish Harlem."

"Clear, sir."

The mayor sat there in disbelief. "How can this son of a bitch keep getting lucky?" he said to himself. He just couldn't understand how every plan they came up with backfired on them. This was going to cost him his career and was his first-class ticket to prison. As he thought about his demise, he noticed the governor flying toward him.

The governor got in the truck and didn't even close the door before he started moving his mouth. "What in the hell happened here, Ralph? I'm hearing both

Speedy and Tuna are dead, and Lucky is nowhere to be found. Please tell me those reports are not accurate."

"I wish I could."

"You wish you could. That's all you can say? I risked my neck helping you in this final fantasy of yours. We broke a lot of rules to get them out of jail. We promised the public that these police officers would be under our watch at their own homes. Explain how in the world they were both found dead on 102nd Street."

"I don't know, and I don't give a fuck. I already killed myself by blowing this last opportunity. Lucky will now disappear. He has gotten his revenge and killed all his ex-partners. He won't stick around. I'm fucked."

"We both are," the governor said.

"Look around. I'm the one that fucked up. What am I going to say to the city now? Once this nonsense hits the news, I'm dead. Not more than twenty-four hours after those three dead bodies in Harlem, we have two more cops. That's a total of five dead cops, three of them feds. All the murders are connected to Lucky. Everything happened within a week. One fuckin' week!"

"I'm going to make some phone calls and start kissing ass now. I'll see you in the morning. Don't be hard on yourself. You always had the city's best interest. Once your laundry hits the media, it's hard to move forward without scrutiny." The governor hugged his political friend.

"Thanks. I'll be okay. I just know I hear the fat lady loud and clear. Don't forget to stop by in the morning. I'm going to stick around for the media and give them my last report. I'm sure I'll be asked to resign."

The governor left with a clear understanding that it was every man for himself. He started making his calls to clear his name and slam the mayor under the bus.

Plus, he didn't like his attitude and sensed he was quitting. Quitters usually started snitching.

As the mayor watched him walk away, he quickly called up Anita Flowers.

"Hello."

"Mrs. Flowers, it's the mayor."

"I know, sir. Please call me Anita."

"I need you on 102nd Street and Lexington Avenue."

"I'm on 108th Street and Lexington Avenue. Once I saw it on the news, I got dressed and jumped in a cab. I should be there in five minutes. Have you made a statement?"

"No, that's why I'm calling, Anita."

"Okay, sir, just send a police captain out to the media. Have him tell them a statement from the mayor is coming within minutes. I'll be there to handle it."

"Sounds great. Please hurry," he said as he hung up. It was a blessing to have Anita's help. He didn't have the right energy to face the media. His behavior would have been out of line.

Within minutes, Anita arrived and was quickly updated on the situation. Without hesitation, she turned around and walked straight to the podium.

As Anita played her role, the mayor disappeared, jumping in his ride and heading down to his office. He needed peace and quiet, and that was usually the only place where he could find it. Both his personal and business phones were ringing, but he ignored them as he sat there in complete silence.

Chapter 14

Little Rock, Arkansas

Lucky was sitting at a Popeyes on 125th Street and Park Avenue. It was going on six o'clock, and he didn't have time to waste. He calmly bit into his chicken. While he ate his food, his brain was racing with different emotions.

The first thing on the list was a car. It was too risky to pull off a carjacking. He had to steal one quietly. By the time the owners realized their car was stolen, he should be halfway to Arkansas, a sixteen- to eighteen-hour drive.

After he finished his food, he jumped in a cab, headed toward the Bronx, to the Yankee Stadium area, figuring that would be a great area to take a car. On his way there, he saw a used car lot and asked the cabdriver to stop.

"Let me out right here."

"Are you sure?" the cabdriver asked.

"I'm positive. Here, keep the change," Lucky said as he handed him a twenty.

Lucky jumped out of the cab and ran across the street. When he walked toward one of the cars for sale, a Hispanic male came out of the little trailer they called an office.

"What's up, *papi?* What kind of car you looking for? My name is Pedro. I'm your man."

Lucky was relieved Pedro knew English. He threw on his acting suit and came up with a story. "Look, Pedro, I'm not going to lie. I have a family issue I need to attend to down in Virginia. I need a car."

"Well, you came to the right place."

"Pedro, here is the deal. I only have cash, no ID. I just need a car for a few days."

"Well, hello, Mr. Cash. How about I let you rent a car and you leave a deposit? Which car you want?"

"I'm looking at that black Explorer with the light tints."

"For how many days you need the truck, Mr. Cash?"

"I need the truck for a week. Just let me know how much it's going to cost to rent it and the deposit."

"I want a thousand to rent for a week and another five thousand for deposit, *papi*. You bring truck back in same condition, I give money back. Any damages, I will keep money. We got a deal?" Pedro extended his hand.

"We got a deal. I'm going to give you ten thousand dollars. When I bring the truck back, just give me back five thousand dollars. You are doing me a big-time favor."

The transaction was a win-win situation for both of them. Pedro bought the truck at an auction for only thirty-eight hundred dollars, so he had nothing to lose if Lucky didn't bring it back. He was going to make a profit, regardless. Lucky leaving ten thousand dollars in total made the deal even sweeter.

For Lucky, he bought himself a ride with no paperwork, and it only cost him ten thousand.

Lucky waited as Pedro changed the oil and fixed up some minor issues, like the brake light and car radio. The Explorer truck was a 2006 model, so Lucky felt comfortable it would be able to handle the long trip.

"Hey, Pedro, let me sit in one of these cars to count the money."

"Go in my office. It's going to take me another fifteen minutes to finish up."

That was exactly what Lucky wanted to hear. Pedro fell in his trap.

Lucky didn't need to count his money, since most of it was already in ten-thousand-dollar bundles. He wanted to get in his office and look around to see if he could find Pedro's personal information.

As soon as Lucky went in the trailer, he found bank statements right on the small desk. He grabbed one of the statements, memorized the address, and placed it back on the desk. He came out of the trailer just as Pedro finished working on the car.

"Just in time, Mr. Cash. The car is ready, and it has a full tank of gas as well."

"Great. Hey, listen. Just so that we understand each other, this meeting never took place. We never met."

"No worries, *papi*. I don't know you."

"Just to make sure, let me make a call." Lucky pulled out his cell phone and acted as if he dialed a legit number. "Hey, it's me," he said. "Listen, if anything happens to me, and I don't come back, pay a visit to Pedro Soto, nineteen-forty-two Sedgwick Avenue, apartment four-b." Lucky then hung up.

"How did you get my address? You were in my office, snooping around?"

"Listen, I'm leaving you with ten thousand dollars. I just want to make sure, when I leave the lot, you don't report the car stolen."

Pedro didn't like it but understood. "Hey, *papi*, I'm a man about my word. No worries. Have a safe trip, and I will see you in a week."

Lucky pulled out of the parking lot, jumped on the George Washington Bridge, and headed toward Little Rock. As he drove, he thought about what he would do to Diamond once he found her. He knew she didn't steal the money, but she was still responsible for calling the cops on him.

In reality, the only thing Diamond did wrong was not go down to Maryland. She decided to go back home and reunite with her family. She wasn't about to be stuck in Maryland all by herself. She knew Lucky was never coming back. She felt she was grown and strong enough to face her family again.

Unfortunately for Diamond, Lucky blamed her for everything. He was going to torture her to death, worse than Sergio. That was how much hate he had for Diamond.

As he drove, he would tighten his grip on the steering wheel. It was beyond frustration. It really hurt him, because he fell in love with her and never would have thought she would drop dime on him. All he kept thinking was, Why couldn't she just leave and go back home? Why would she call the cops on him and cause all the additional headaches?

The mayor was back at his office, still in a daze. His secretary kept screening his calls and taking messages. She even stopped going in the office, because he kept yelling at her every time she went in.

After the governor never got any of his messages returned, he decided to show up at his office. As soon as he turned the knob, he heard a single shot come from inside the mayor's office. The governor ran in to find the mayor's head lying on his desk. He had killed himself with a single shot to his temple with a .38 special. The governor instructed the secretary to call 9-1-1. He checked for a pulse. "C'mon, Ralph," he said, "you have a family. You can't check out like this."

The governor stood back and let the medical staff do their job. He was staring at Ralph, as his own life flashed in front of him. He was hoping he didn't have to commit suicide. It was sad and a low point in the governor's career, but if he played his cards right, he could come out on top. He was going to use the mayor's suicide to his advantage and play the blame game.

The city didn't have too much sympathy for its mayor. In all reality, the majority of New Yorkers didn't care and only felt sorry for his family. They all agreed the mayor took the easy way out, instead of suffering in jail like the criminal he was. A lot of lives were lost under his watch, which could have been prevented. The whispers in the streets were all the same. Everyone was ready for a new voice. They needed a leader with a clean background and fresh ideas that would bring the glory back to New York.

The next twelve hours for New Yorkers felt more like twenty-two hours. The mayor's entire dirty laundry was made public, as all the accusations Lucky brought to light were now being revisited by the federal government. Some felt it was a waste of time because the mayor was dead and couldn't defend himself, just like the commissioner.

Reporter Destine Diaz had reported that she had learned from a reliable source that the mayor was the one who had the commissioner assassinated. Her accusations raised some eyebrows and got her suspended from her job. She was only reporting what Richard Claiborne made her aware of. Destine didn't have any evidence to back up her story. Her only hope was if they captured Richard. Then he would come clean. But, knowing the CIA, she thought they would probably kill him to keep his mouth shut forever.

Thirteen hours into his trip, Lucky decided to pull over and catch about an hour of sleep. He had driven through the night, stopping only for gas and snacks, and was tired. His eyes were starting to hurt, and he couldn't keep them open.

With so much on his mind, Lucky couldn't rest. After about thirty minutes of tossing back and forth in the driver's seat, he'd had enough. He went in the bathroom, washed his face, and got himself a large coffee and two five-hour energies. Within minutes, around ten in the morning, he was back on the highway, with another five to six hours to go.

Back in New York, all the morning stations and national media outlets were reporting the mayor's suicide and his alleged involvement in the commissioner's assassination. Some media outlets mentioned that the CIA was involved to some degree, but no one could verify it.

Then, there was Lucky's mysterious disappearance. It still baffled the public that he wasn't captured. That was why he was labeled the American bin Laden. New Yorkers, at the end of the day, loved Lucky. They just didn't like the amount of dead bodies they claimed he was responsible for, especially that female found tied up and shot.

That raised the question of him being set up. Maybe the police department wanted payback because he exposed their dirty deeds.

Lucky was the number one enemy among the boys in blue. From the moment he'd testified, every police officer in the world had hated him. You didn't cross the line. That was worse than working with Internal Affairs.

New Yorkers understood how much he was hated. They were assuming he was framed. The public just wanted to hear from Lucky himself to make an independent judgment.

Back at the Colemans', a bit of a celebration was taking place. Laura Coleman had had her wish granted. She wanted all the officers charged with her son's murder dead and didn't feel one ounce of sympathy for them or their families, because the same courtesy wasn't extended to her.

Before Lucky came forward, it was believed that her son indeed had a gun on him when he was killed. They began calling her son a criminal, saying he was armed and dangerous. Laura knew better and pleaded with the public to hold back judgment on her son's character. She knew he was innocent and didn't shoot at the officers, as alleged.

If it wasn't for Lucky, the truth would have never been revealed. Laura questioned her faith throughout the ordeal, but she still prayed every night before going to bed. That same ole prayer she recited had a new name added, which she always thanked as well. *Lucky.*

***

Not everybody was ready to label Lucky a misunderstood hero. The governor was still on the hunt and made it part of his business to continue tracking down Lucky. His department reached out to the CIA, and after numerous attempts, he was able to track down Agent Scott Meyer.

"Hello, this is the governor. Are you still on the line, Agent Meyer?"

"Yes, sir. How can I help you? How did you find me?"

"C'mon, just because the FBI and CIA personally don't like each other doesn't mean we don't have friends in each other's departments."

"True. So how can I help you?"

"I understand you visited the mayor on a few occasions. I want to know the business behind those meetings."

"I can't disclose that information. That was between the mayor and us."

"Well, how about I release your name and your pretty little partner's name to the media?"

"Okay, listen, let's meet in about an hour. I will give you what I have. I think we know where Lucky is heading to."

"Now, that sounds a lot better. I will be waiting on your call."

The governor was excited that he was going to receive exclusive information about Lucky's whereabouts. Catching Lucky would help him in his bid to run for the presidency down the road. He couldn't wait until the meeting with Agent Meyer.

The past few weeks had been the most challenging of the governor's career. The only good out of it was, all parties involved in the corruption plot were now dead. It would be easy to start all over. Besides, his name never came up. For the time being, until the new acting mayor was appointed, Governor Andrew Silver was taking over all responsibilities.

After all the alleged corrupt officials were dead, there was a collective sigh of relief all around the streets. The healing process was going to take time. Many were not fully recovered from the riots yet, but at least the worst rogue cops in the NYPD's history were now gone.

By the time the six o'clock news came on, the tone of the broadcast had changed. Only ten minutes of their sixty-minute segment was spent on the mayor and the dead officers. The media was trying to help New Yorkers forget about the drama.

It was going on seven in the evening, and Lucky was staying at a crappy motel off Willow Mills Highway in Little Rock, five minutes away from the address Asia gave him. He was unaware of what was going on back in New York, and he didn't care. All he was concerned with was taking out Diamond and getting back to his family.

Lucky got dressed and packed up like he was gone for the night, even though the room was paid up for three more days. Though he was just going to do a routine stakeout first, he knew there was a possibility he might not return to the room.

Diamond's family lived in a house on S. Chester Street and Wright. He drove over there and parked down the street. He noticed a white two-door Mercedes with temporary tags. He knew that was Diamond's car. The one she used to always talk about when they were together.

Lucky was out there for at least three hours before he saw any movement. Someone turned on the light on the front porch. He sat up. He saw someone come out of the house, but by the time he tried to get a closer look, they had already jumped in the white Benz.

He started following the car. In his mind, it could only be Diamond. He followed the car for about ten minutes and ended up in a quiet, fancier neighborhood. When the white Benz parked, Lucky parked as well and kept watching. The driver jumped out, and it was Diamond.

Lucky paused. He had to catch his breath, and himself. He wanted to jump on her right in the parking lot. He decided he would wait and see which building she walked into, and after that, watch which lights she turned on. Once he saw which apartment she was staying in, he would make his move and ambush her ass.

It was going on two in the morning, and everything was going according to plan. He knew which apartment she lived in, and he waited until the lights went off. Lucky finally decided to make his move, slowly walking in the apartment building and up the stairs to the second floor.

As Lucky attempted to unlock the door, out of nowhere, it swung open. It was Diamond standing by the front door.

"About time you fuckin' found me," she said. "What? You didn't think I knew you were following me? Don't forget, you taught me all the tricks. Come here, baby," Diamond said, not knowing Lucky was actually there to kill her. Once she saw Lucky standing there, it meant the world to her. She thought he was there to reclaim her as his woman.

Lucky slapped her so hard, he lifted her body off the floor, and she landed flat on her back.

She grabbed her face. "What the fuck was that for? You can't be mad that I didn't go to Maryland."

"Oh, you think I'm just mad about that? Is there something else you want to tell me?" Lucky went to slap her again.

"Wait, baby. Just wait. What are you talking about?"

"I'm talking about the fuckin' cops raiding my storage facility. You didn't have anything to do with that?" he said as he cocked back his gun.

"I swear to fuckin' God I didn't. So, now you are going to shoot me, Lucky? What the fuck!"

Lucky knew when Diamond was lying. He tried to read her and felt like she was telling the truth. That was puzzling. He'd believed in his heart Diamond was the one who snitched.

"Listen, Lucky, when I left that night for Maryland, I actually went to Sergio's apartment. I didn't want to go to Maryland and be alone. Fuck that! I decided to come back home. I felt I was strong enough to face my demons. That's all I did. Why would I call the cops on the love of my life?"

"Maybe you were mad because I sent you down there without me. I don't fuckin' know. All I know is, my spot got raided, and all signs point to you. You better come up with a better story than that, bitch."

"Bitch? How dare you call me that! Now you are disrespecting me, Lucky?"

"So I'm supposed to believe you stayed at Sergio's apartment a few days and nothing happened?"

"Whatever. You don't fuckin' believe me, let's call Sergio."

"We don't have to. I already confronted Sergio about that."

"Well then, you know I'm telling the truth. Why you all in my face like that, Lucky? Like I'm a fuckin' mark. That's how you treating me."

"If you was a mark, you would have been dead already, but we can't call him, anyway."

"You killed him? Why? Sergio didn't do anything. I was at his apartment for a few days, and that man never attempted anything. He had too much respect for you. Oh Lawd, you killed Sergio. He was like a son to you."

"Why everybody keeps fuckin' saying that? He wasn't my son. When I went to visit him, the CIA was leaving his apartment. I'm assuming they traced the call and that's how they found him. The call was made from Sergio's phone, so if you didn't, then who? According to my sources, it was a female who made the call."

"I don't know. I didn't. That's all that should count. I seen this look before. It's the same look before you pull off a job. You're making me nervous."

"You should be, because I didn't drive all the way down here for hugs and kisses. I want the truth. You should be a real woman and own up to it."

"Nigga, please. I'm a woman. A real one who will never double-cross her man. If the call came from Sergio's phone, then maybe he had his girl call."

"That's a possibility, but all signs still point toward you," Lucky said as he picked her up from the floor. "Sit over there on the sofa. We're going to get to the bottom of this."

"C'mon, baby, why would I call the cops on you? It doesn't make sense. You saved my life, Lucky. I owe you more than my life. Yes, I was mad that you left me, but that doesn't mean I want you in jail for life. I have to respect the fact that you wanted to get your family back. I know your daughter means everything to you. I can't come between that. Fuck your baby mama! But I knew that's what you wanted. It didn't matter how many nights I woke up with a soaked pillow, crying my eyes out. I think about you every day, Lucky. I thought you changed your mind and came back for me. I guess I was wrong."

"Whatever. If you love me like you say you do, then you would have followed the plan and went down to Maryland. Why come back here to your hometown?"

"Because this is all I know."

"What? Being abused is all you know? When you left, you were a little girl. Now you are a grown woman. You had the opportunity to start a fresh life somewhere else. Why come here, where it all went wrong?"

"I know, but I didn't want a fresh start. What part of *you were my all* don't you understand? Remember, you left me and lied to me. You weren't going to meet me in Maryland. Let's be honest with each other."

"You didn't know that. I'm not going to lie. I didn't have intentions of coming back at first. When you left that day, well, when I thought you left, I was down. I couldn't stop thinking about you. I was going to wait a few months before I popped up. I love you too much to abandon you."

Lucky pulled out some handcuffs and cuffed her to one of her kitchen chairs. He moved her to a corner far away from any objects she might use as a weapon. After he secured her, he sat across from her and stared at her. He was really stuck on killing her. He didn't know what to do. She sounded believable, but he'd already reached the point of no return. If he let her walk away, he would second-guess himself for life.

It didn't help Diamond's situation that she was most likely there when Sergio made the call. An angry black woman's revenge was the number one fear among black men. They would do the unthinkable.

Diamond sat there quietly. She couldn't believe Lucky just popped up out of nowhere. She never thought he would find her here. As bad as she talked about her family, it was the last place she thought he would check. She didn't like how Lucky was looking at her. She knew she was in trouble.

"So, are you just going to stare at me?" she said to break the ice.

"I'm just thinking. That's all."

"About what?" She licked her lips. "How much you miss me?"

"Please, girl, that sweet talk is not going to help you today. I'm trying to decide if you should live or die."

Diamond exhaled and looked at Lucky. "You have to believe me. I didn't call the cops, and I didn't know Sergio called the cops. Baby, you have to believe me."

Lucky didn't reply. He continued sitting there in silence.

Originally, he wanted to torture her so bad, her mother wouldn't have been able to identify her. He had about a hundred different ways to make her suffer and die slowly. He thought about locking her in a room with two hungry and mad-as-shit pit bulls while she was handcuffed.

Then he started thinking about how much he loved her. All recent memories with Diamond were good ones. Truth be told, he wasn't going back for Tasha. It had always been about Tamika. If he could swap baby mamas, he would. He was disappointed that she didn't go to Maryland and at least try. He'd spent money on the house and given her a hundred thousand.

Lucky had to take a deep breath. He was starting to get upset. He caught himself before he started getting mad.

"C'mon, Lucky, say something, my love. Why are you doing this? For real, why?"

"It's the trust issue, Dee. You sound believable, but I don't feel right. It's a hole in the story, and I can't pinpoint it. I'm just waiting to see it if comes to me."

"C'mon, let me go, Lucky. You know in your heart I didn't do nothing."

"I wouldn't go that far. The whole Sergio situation is throwing me off."

"I'm telling you, baby. Nothing happened between Sergio and I. The only thing he did was encourage me to go back home."

"Encourage you? What you mean?" Lucky said as he sat up.

"Calm down, honey. I told him about our situation, and he agreed it was a little fucked up, and that I should do what's best for me. You had too much heat on you," Diamond said, feeling a bit more comfortable. She saw it in his eyes. He wasn't going to kill her. He was just trying to scare her, and it was working.

"So, it was Sergio's idea for you to come back home?"

"No, but something like that."

Lucky stood up, cocked back his 9-millimeter, pointed it at Diamond, and aimed for her head.

Diamond still wasn't alarmed about it. There was no way he was serious.

"It's about trust. I always want to feel like I could trust you." Lucky blew her a kiss. Then he shot her twice, knocking her backward.

She ended up in a sitting position with her legs up, blood leaking from the two holes in her head, and her eyes open.

Lucky kneeled down and closed them for her. He kissed his index and middle finger and touched her forehead. "I will always love you, baby."

He got up and quickly ran the hell up out of there. He couldn't believe he'd just pulled the trigger. He felt like he was left with no options. Diamond was cuffed, but his hands were tied behind him as well. If he let her live, then he wouldn't get an opportunity to make a clean move forward. She would always be in the middle. He needed her out of the picture. He did think about letting her slide, but when she said Sergio encouraged her to move back home, the trust issue came to mind again. He just could not risk her living and knowing his past, if he was going to move forward. She could still be an informant.

Lucky's decision to go back to Tasha and his daughter was Diamond's death certificate. She didn't move down to Maryland as planned and stayed a few days at Sergio the snitch's house. She just couldn't be trusted, so she had to die.

He jumped in the black Explorer and found his way back to the highway. He was moving fast because he felt like maybe a neighbor or two could have been looking out the window when he peeled off. If the police showed up, he would be long gone.

As he was driving, tears were coming down his face. He didn't want to kill Diamond, but it was what it was. He'd created her, so he felt like he could destroy her. Once he reunited with his family, he would get a fresh start, and Diamond, along with his ex-partners, would all become a distant memory. To start his new life, all he would need was plastic surgery to change his look.

He reached for his phone and started calling Tasha. Speaking to her would make him forget about Diamond.

She picked up on the second ring. "Hello. Please tell me you are on your way," Tasha said in excitement.

"I'm on my way. I should be there in another six to seven hours."

"Please don't bullshit me. I don't have time for any new games, Lucky."

"Why would I play like that? It's all over. I will be there. Please, tell my li'l princess the king will be there soon."

"I sure will. But what about the queen? I don't get any special shout-outs? I've been waiting for this moment for a very long time."

"I have something special planned for the two of us. Don't worry, sweetheart. Now you have me until I grow old. I will never leave your side again."

"I love you, Lucky. Drive safely. Oh, I almost forgot to tell you. The mayor committed suicide."

"Get the fuck out of here! He did? That's great news. Ha! So he pulled the trigger on himself. What a coward! Thanks for the news. You just made my ride a better one. I will see you in a few."

Lucky hung up the phone, happy to hear the mayor was dead. That meant everyone involved in the corruption allegations was gone. It worked out perfect, almost like he drew it out. He'd never expected to kill Diamond, but casualties were a part of the game. It got to the point where he was starting to believe his luck was running out. Now, after a few close calls with death, he still didn't know how he was able to escape all the drama unhurt.

As he drove, he tried to stay awake by counting how many blue cars he passed. Lucky couldn't get Diamond or Haze out of his mind, the only two individuals who he wished didn't get caught in the cross fire. He felt bad for Diamond only because he truly loved her. He just couldn't accept that there was a possibility that she'd indeed snitched.

On the other hand, he really felt fucked up about Haze. Even though Haze picked his own destiny, Lucky still felt awful. Haze had made up his mind, but Lucky didn't step up and make him change it, like he did when Haze was talking about killing his baby mama. Crossed by his associates in the past, Lucky had a feeling Haze would have been by far the most loyal. It was too bad he was gone, leaving another single black mother to raise his family.

Once Lucky was back with Tasha, he planned to hit up Asia and find out Haze's real name and address. He would send like a hundred thousand dollars. It wouldn't bring Haze back, but it would help his family get through the hard times.

Chapter 15

Finally Reunited with Tamika

It was going on noon, and Lucky was about five minutes away from hugging his wifey and daughter. It was a long time coming for that moment. He'd had many sweaty nights when he felt like that day would never arrive. He called Tasha.

"Where are you, Lucky?"

"Damn! A simple hello would have been better."

"Whatever. I've been waiting on you all this time. Where are you, honey? Stop playing. I've been a nervous wreck since you called and said you hours away from us."

"I'm at the gas station."

"What the fuck for, Lucky?"

"Calm down. The gas tank is on empty. I wanted to put some gas in it. I'm not parking the truck with no gas, just in case I have to make a run for it."

"Okay, but hurry up. We'll be waiting outside for you. Tamika has been up since, like, five this morning, waiting for you. I don't know who's more excited between the both of us."

"No one is more excited than I am. I'm in a black Ford Explorer. I should be pulling up soon. Don't wait outside. It will bring attention."

"Why not?" a curious Tasha asked.

"Baby, don't wait outside. We don't need the extra attention."

"Okay, I will just look out the window, then," she said, disappointed.

"Did you cook?"

"You know I did. I made one of your favorites, but hurry up and get your butt over here before I throw it in the garbage."

"Yeah, right. Here I come."

Lucky hung up the phone, smiling ear to ear, but still looking over his shoulder. He couldn't forget the *America's Most Wanted* piece they did on him. He had to be cautious. Two million dollars would give an old dude 20/20 vision.

After filling up the tank, which cost almost seventy dollars, he jumped in and headed to his family. As he pulled into the gated community, he parked his truck and jumped out. He got out and could see both Tasha and Tamika waving from the window like he was the first human contact they had seen in years. That made him smile and wave back.

After Lucky went to the back to retrieve his bag, he started walking toward the front door. He looked back up at the window to see Tamika blowing him kisses. Lucky so happened to look up toward the roof and noticed what looked like a marksman. Before he could even react, two loud shots erupted in that quiet community.

Bang! Bang!

Lucky dropped to the ground after getting shot twice in the head.

Both Tasha and Tamika began yelling and crying. At first they felt like they were daydreaming. When Tasha realized it wasn't a bad dream, that Lucky was actually shot, she asked her mom to hold Tamika and she flew down the steps. When she made it to her man, he was dead. There was blood everywhere.

Tasha started yelling, hoping someone would call 9-1-1. "No! Oh my God! Please don't do this to us. Oh God! Please help! Someone help!" She looked up at the window and could see and hear Tamika still screaming for her father.

Tasha grabbed Lucky around his neck and lifted his head up. She wanted to make sure he was dead and there was nothing for him to say. While doing that, she noticed the bag he was carrying. She grabbed it and put it behind her back. She knew it was stuffed with money, because that was one of the main reasons he went back to New York.

Within a few minutes, there were police officers everywhere. Tasha started looking around, and when she saw what looked like FBI agents on the scene, she put one and one together and knew the feds must have assassinated him. She ran upstairs, grabbed a few things, and told her mother and Tamika they were leaving.

"Mom, wait a second! What happened to my father? Is he dead?" a hysterical Tamika asked.

"Now is not the time to talk about it."

"But, Mom, that's Daddy. They shot him in front of us. Who would want to kill my father? I want to see him. Please, take me downstairs. I want to see him. Please, Mother, please," Tamika begged.

"Listen, Tamika, your father was a wanted man. He did some bad things that we can't discuss right now. I'm sorry I never told you the truth about him."

"So he wasn't a cop?" she asked and started wiping her tears.

"No, that part is true. He just wasn't a good one. We will talk later. I promise I will sit you down and explain everything. Right now is not the time. We need to disappear before they come after us."

"But why? I don't understand."

"Girl, just bring your ass and stop asking so many fuckin' questions." Tasha had to pause. She had never lost her cool and cursed at Tamika. "Listen, I'm sorry for cursing. Your father sacrificed his life in order for no one to know our true identities. He arrested powerful, bad people who usually go after the family of the arresting cops. Your daddy never told anyone about us. Now they have found him. I'm sure they want to look for us. No more questions. I'm sorry you just witnessed the murder of your father, but we have to go."

"Okay, Mommy." Tamika ran back toward the window. Her father's lifeless body was still lying on the ground. She blew her daddy a kiss. "Thank you for giving up you life for me. I love you. God will protect you."

Tasha, her mother, and Tamika disappeared through the back entrance of the three-story building. Tasha didn't pack any clothes. She just grabbed her money and the money she snatched from Lucky. She always parked her car out of sight just in case she had to make a quick getaway.

Tasha thought she was getting away, not realizing the feds had been watching her for two days now. As she was driving out of the gated community, one of the SWAT members radioed in to find out if they should stop them.

"Sir, come in. This is Captain Ortiz."

"Yes, Captain," Governor Andrew Silver said.

"The target's girlfriend is trying to make a getaway."

"Pull her over and hit me on the radio."

"Affirmative."

The governor, along with the CIA, was able to track down Lucky's family. When the CIA had visited Sergio before Lucky killed him, Sergio told them the number Lucky gave him when he asked him to call Tasha. The

CIA was able to trace the cell, and that was how they found Tasha. When Lucky called her and told her he would be on his way, they were waiting for him as well.

The governor gave one order—kill him on sight. They weren't going to give him another opportunity to escape.

"Sir, come in."

"Yes, Captain Ortiz," the governor shot back.

"We have detained the target's family."

"Okay, Captain, put the radio near the girlfriend's ear."

"They can hear you, sir."

"Good. I'm going to make this short. A lot of people have died and suffered because of Lucky and his ex-partners. We are not going to hold anything against you. We're sorry you had to witness what you saw. Enjoy your fresh start. Captain Ortiz, let them go." The governor turned off his radio.

Even though the governor hated Lucky, he wasn't a monster. He wasn't about to ruin their lives. Since Lucky's ex-partners' families were left alone, he decided to give Tasha the same courtesy.

Tasha was scared to death and didn't know what to expect. When she heard they could leave, she put the car in drive and peeled off. She didn't even look through the rearview mirror. She jumped on the highway and headed to Florida.

The governor was at the crime scene, staring at Lucky. He couldn't understand why that pig was so hard to find. In a way, he was glad he'd exposed corruption in the city.

The governor headed to the airport, on his way back to New York, where he would be labeled a hero. The news traveled fast, and all the news stations were reporting the death of Lucky. It was big news. A lot celebrated, some cried, but a breath of fresh air was felt throughout the gritty streets of New York.

Destine Diaz was sitting on her sofa, sipping coffee. The longer she stayed out of work, the more depressed she became. TV was her life, and she didn't have a backup plan. It was going on six o'clock in the evening when her doorman buzzed her from downstairs.

Destine was short. "Yes, Fred?"

"I'm sorry to bother you, but you have a package."

"A package this late? From whom?"

"It just says, 'To Destine Diaz from Donald Gibson.'"

Destine spat the coffee out of her mouth. "What name did you just say?"

"Donald Gibson," the doorman repeated.

"Please, bring it up. I'll be by the elevator."

When the elevator doors opened, Destine was waiting in anticipation. She was so excited, she'd walked out in her T-shirt and panties.

Fred was taken aback. "This package must be pretty important," he said, looking at her up and down.

When Destine realized what the hell she'd just done, she snatched the package and ran back in the condo. Right before she closed the door, she yelled to Fred, "I'm sure this package will get me my job back!"

Destine went in her living room and leaned against the door. She couldn't believe she'd just walked out in her underwear. Her face was red with embarrassment. Good thing Fred was in his sixties and a gentleman.

She ripped open the package and found a DVD disc and a note inside. The note read:

Destine

It's me, Lucky. The DVD, it's an interview I recorded. I wanted you to interview me, but with all the drama going on, it was impossible. On this disc, you have my confession, and you have my life. I just want to ask for one favor. Don't play this until after I'm killed. I might be dead by the time you get this DVD, anyway, so it wouldn't even matter. I just want New York to hear my side of the story.

Lucky

A tear came down Destine's eye. She could only imagine what was on the DVD. She felt honored that Lucky chose her and had faith in her abilities.

She popped in the DVD. Once she confirmed it was Lucky, she stopped it and called her boss. She didn't even get a chance to see the whole story. When she told him she had Lucky's video confession, he offered her job back with a few extra perks. Destine accepted his offer over the phone and headed down to the station, where they were going to broadcast live at eight instead of ten o'clock.

The news station was already promoting the breaking news. Once New Yorkers heard they had a video of Lucky confessing to his wrongdoings, it caught everyone's attention. No one had ever heard his side of the story, except maybe those present at the Coleman trial. Plus, so much had happened since the trial. Everyone was eager to hear his side.

When Destine arrived at the station, it was going on seven thirty. She quickly gave the DVD to her production team while makeup was being applied. The news of her firing was made public, so New Yorkers would be shocked to see her back in front of the camera.

Destine didn't lose a beat. She was prepared like the veteran she was. As eight o'clock rolled around, she was back in the limelight.

"Good evening, New York. Thank you for tuning in at this special time for this exclusive interview we have with Donald 'Lucky' Gibson. Today, around six this evening, I received a package, a DVD, from Lucky with a note that read, 'I know I'm going to get killed. Please make sure you play this DVD.'

Ladies and gentlemen, here we go. If you have young children, please use your own discretion, but I wouldn't let my children watch this clip."

"Hello, everyone, if you are watching this video, then you all are aware that I'm dead. I recorded this because I wanted an opportunity to say my side. I know these past few weeks have been a nightmare for all of us. Throughout these allegations, I have been silent. The time has come for me to clear my name in some of these allegations made against me. I know nothing I say will change the past. Heck, it won't even bring me back to life. I just want to get the opportunity to rest in peace, so I'm cleansing my soul.

"I first want to touch a li'l bit about myself and why I became a police officer. I was raised by a single mother. I never once met my father. My mother did an excellent job in raising me. I was able to stay out of trouble, though I had no father figure in my life. I had an opportunity to become either a baseball or football player. I rejected all kinds of scholarships to play for national schools. I wanted to stay close to home and be with my mother.

"I was raised with great morals and respect, so I just thought it was the right thing to do and join the police academy. I always wondered why there weren't any black cops in my neighborhood, so I wanted to make a difference and show the rest of my community that it was okay to become a cop. After my mother was killed by a drunk driver, it changed my life for the worse.

My morals died with my mother. I still followed my dreams of becoming an officer to keep my mother happy, but the passion was not there.

"After joining the force, the first few years, everything went as expected. I was getting promoted left and right for my outstanding achievements. I did everything by the book. I was the perfect cop, and everyone in my neighborhood loved me. Once I became a detective and I joined the elite unit called Operation Clean House, everything went wrong. The unit was run by Captain Tuna, and then it was Detective Loose Cannon, Speedy, and Tango. Tuna was the captain, but the real brain behind it all was Commissioner Fratt. At first I dealt with the pressure of being the only black man in the unit. As time went on, I just adapted, and the dirty tactics became second nature. I honestly thought, in order to close some of these cases, we had to play criminals. We put away some very dangerous men. I can't lie. I saw how easy we were getting away with the illegal shit we were doing. I got greedy and started committing crimes on my own. I was making a lot of money. That's how I opened up the storage facility in the Bronx along with my dead associates Divine, Pee-Wee, and Blood. We were a deadly force in the streets.

"I'm not proud of what I'm here revealing today. I just want to get the truth out. After one of my partners in the unit, Tango, was set up and killed in one of our undercover missions, I became suspicious. I thought Tango's murder was in-house. I bugged my own team. I knew we were a dirty unit, but I knew it went deeper than just the commissioner. That's when I found out the damn mayor was the king of the mud. I became my own internal affair team, keeping all evidence instead of destroying it. I was going to put

all the files together and submit them to the federal government and the media.

"After putting together my plan to come forward and confess, I suffered a setback. My ex-partners decided to kill an innocent black man just because he blew our high. We were on the job, snorting cocaine and hanging out at a strip club. Well, once I heard the murder charges were about to get dropped against my ex-partners, I stepped forward and decided to testify.

"Once I took that stand, my life became a nightmare. I was the number one target. First, my ex-partners tried to kill me in broad daylight in Central Park. They thought I was meeting with the Colemans and I sent a look-alike, a stunt double, you can say. They killed him on sight.

"Then they hired a crew of contract bounty hunters out of Florida. They kill their targets. There were, like, four of them. They were good, but not that good. However, they figured out I had a female companion with me, which is true. Once she became a target, I came up with the story of a young girl turning herself in. Now, I'm going to admit I made a crucial decision that I had to live with. I shot and killed an innocent woman. I did it because I wanted to save the identity of my female protégée, who I was in love with.

"After she disappeared as planned, that's when the folders were coming to light. Everything was going well until they found where my baby mother and daughter lived in Cape Cod. They were seconds away from kidnapping my baby mother. I interfered, and I killed both of them. I know for a fact one of them was a fed. The federal government was now helping my dirty ex-partners and doing it at all costs.

"I gathered up my family, and we all left Cape Cod. I took them somewhere safe. After I returned back to New York, I went to my storage unit, and that's when we had the face-off with police. Snipers killed my friend Divine, while the police burned up my other friend, Pee-Wee. I was able to escape, and I stayed over a friend's house to lay low.

"I passed out on the roof, high off cocaine 'cause I relapsed, and then the king of all corruption, the commissioner, gets assassinated. Then, minutes later, they are blaming me for it. I run down to Maryland, where I was trapped in a hotel. I shot the police officer only because I knew he had on a vest, nothing personal. If you are watching, I'm sorry. I knew what I was doing. Again, I'm sorry for the bruise.

"After that, I make it back up to New York. I wanted to clear my name and prove I didn't kill the commissioner. In the process, about another ten dead bodies popped up, including the murder of Captain Tuna and Detective Speedy. Another thing, I'm not responsible for the death of those three federal agents in Harlem. Also, if you find Richard Claiborne, the mayor's assistant, you will find out who truly killed the commissioner. I will give you a clue—he runs the city. Once I took care of my ex-partners, the plan was to reunite with my family.

"Before I left, I decided to record this video. If I know the federal government like I do, they are going to kill me. I caused too much embarrassment.

"I want to take this time to thank the people first. I want to apologize to New York. I did the city dirty. I want to apologize to the Colemans. That's one strong family. I'm sorry I couldn't stop them before they killed your son. I'm sorry.

"Now it's time to talk to one special lady out there who I love, my daughter. I'm sorry, baby girl. I'm so sorry."

The tears were flowing once Lucky mentioned his daughter.

"I know I made a promise to my daughter, and if you're hearing this recording, I didn't make it back alive. I'm sorry. You are the last person in the world I wanted to let down. I'm sorry. Please forgive me. Please understand I did it all because of you. I know you are hearing all the news channels talking about your father, and it has you confused. Trust what your mother tells you. She knows the truth. I didn't abandon you, baby. For your safety, your mother moved you away. I was just too stupid to see it back then. I'm going to ask you for one favor, baby girl. Please take good care of your mother. I know she's watching as well.

"What up, baby? You are a great mother. I really wanted to start over and do this family thing with you. I'm sorry. I let cocaine ruin my life and cause pain in yours. I can't believe I let you slip through my fingers. Take care of my daughter, and make sure she grows up to be a woman like you. I have to go now. I love you guys."

He broke down again and could barely speak as he added, *"This is Donald Gibson, better known as, well, I guess not anymore. I guess I wasn't so lucky, after all.*

Good night and God bless ya.

Notes

Notes

ORDER FORM
URBAN BOOKS, LLC
78 E. Industry Ct
Deer Park, NY 11729

Name: (please print):____________________________________

Address: ____________________________________

City/State: ____________________________________

Zip: ____________________________________

QTY	TITLES	PRICE
	The Cartel	$14.95
	The Cartel 2	$14.95
	The Dopeman's Wife	$14.95
	The Prada Plan	$14.95
	Gunz And Roses	$14.95
	Snow White	$14.95
	A Pimp's Life	$14.95
	Hush	$14.95
	Little Black Girl Lost 1	$14.95
	Little Black Girl Lost 2	$14.95
	Little Black Girl Lost 3	$14.95
	Little Black Girl Lost 4	$14.95

Shipping and handling-add $3.50 for 1st book, then $1.75 for each additional book.
Please send a check payable to:
Urban Books, LLC
Please allow 4-6 weeks for delivery

ORDER FORM
URBAN BOOKS, LLC
78 E. Industry Ct
Deer Park, NY 11729

Name: (please print):____________________________________

Address: ____________________________________

City/State: ____________________________________

Zip: ____________________________________

QTY	TITLES	PRICE
	16 ½ On The Block	$14.95
	16 On The Block	$14.95
	Betrayal	$14.95
	Both Sides Of The Fence	$14.95
	Cheesecake And Teardrops	$14.95
	Denim Diaries	$14.95
	Happily Ever Now	$14.95
	Hell Has No Fury	$14.95
	If It Isn't love	$14.95
	Last Breath	$14.95
	Loving Dasia	$14.95
	Say It Ain't So	$14.95

Shipping and handling-add $3.50 for 1st book, then $1.75 for each additional book.
Please send a check payable to:
Urban Books, LLC
Please allow 4-6 weeks for delivery

ORDER FORM
URBAN BOOKS, LLC
78 E. Industry Ct
Deer Park, NY 11729

Name:(please print):___________________________________

Address: ___________________________________

City/State: ___________________________________

Zip: ___________________________________

QTY	TITLES	PRICE
	A Man's Worth	$14.95
	Abundant Rain	$14.95
	Battle Of Jericho	$14.95
	By The Grace Of God	$14.95
	Dance Into Destiny	$14.95
	Divorcing The Devil	$14.95
	Forsaken	$14.95
	Grace And Mercy	$14.95
	Guilty Of Love	$14.95
	His Woman, His Wife, His Widow	$14.95
	Illusions	$14.95
	The LoveChild	$14.95

Shipping and handling-add $3.50 for 1st book, then $1.75 for each additional book.

Please send a check payable to:

Urban Books, LLC

Please allow 4-6 weeks for delivery

ORDER FORM
URBAN BOOKS, LLC
78 E. Industry Ct
Deer Park, NY 11729

Name: (please print):____________________________________

Address: ____________________________________

City/State: ____________________________________

Zip: ____________________________________

QT

Ship ... for
each
Pleas

Pleas